The
DUTTON GIRL

Reviews for
FIRE IN THE RECTORY
**and two more
John Nolan
detective novellas**

★★★★★ – *five out of five stars* "Excellent ... Each tale has twists and turns I could never manage to predict. Was the fire an accident or arson? Is Mr. Hughes truly the sort of man he seems? If the most obvious suspect did indeed commit the murder, where is his weapon? I didn't even try to guess the answers to these questions but merely let the story take me along for the ride."
MANHATTAN BOOK REVIEW

"*Engrossing ... One of Fire in the Rectory's strengths lies in its historical accuracy, which brings the era and its culture to life ... All the stories excel in a fine balance of whodunit, politics, cultural inspection, and a senseof 1900s America.*"
THE MIDWEST BOOK REVIEW

"*Ingenious writing ... Set during the time of World War I when immigrants were arriving in force to the United States, the author shows how bigotry, poverty, and corruption prevailed with his well-researched historical facts.*"
READER VIEWS REVIEW

"Fans of classical detective novels and who-done-its should enjoy these stories ... The period detail is extremely accurate, giving a nice feel of New York in the early 20th century, and photo illustrations add to this sense of the era .... The dialogue is well written, and the plots move along nicely ... Competently crafted."
HISTORICAL NOVELS REVIEW

The
DUTTON GIRL

A John Nolan Detective Novel

STAN FREEMAN

~⚮~

HAMPSHIRE HOUSE PUBLISHING CO.
FLORENCE, MASS.

THE DUTTON GIRL

by Stan Freeman

Hampshire House Publishing Co.

www.hampshirehousepub.com

All photo illustrations are by the author.

Manufactured in the United States of America

ISBN: 978-1-7344384-0-6

THE DUTTON GIRL was originally published by Coffeetown Press of Seattle in June of 2018. This is a republication of the title in 2020 by Hampshire House Publishing Co.

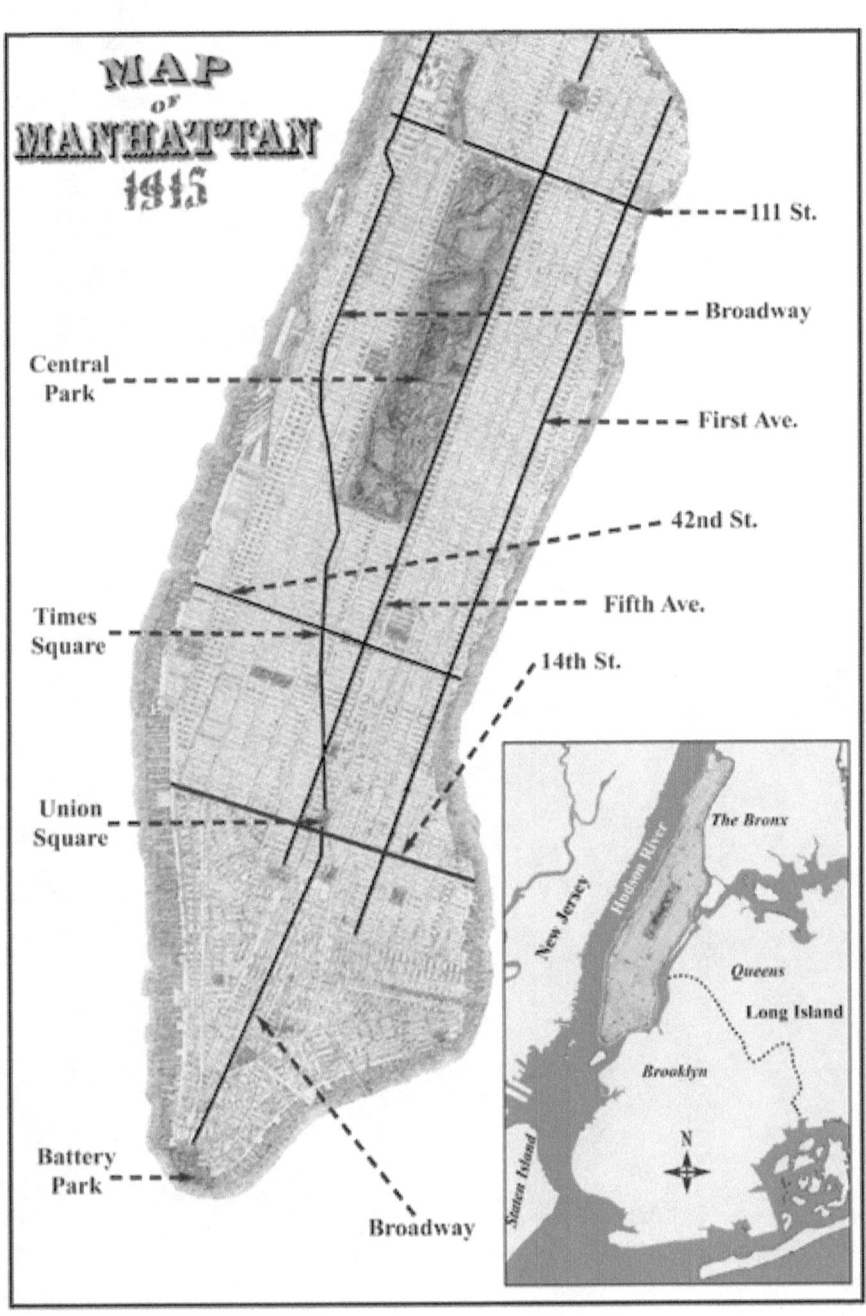

Table of Contents

Sarah Dutton

1

The Crime

∾

SARAH WILLINGHAM DUTTON joined other prominent young women of Manhattan society on the afternoon of December nineteenth, 1914, at Grand Central Palace, an exhibition hall on 46th Street.

With the war raging in Europe, a war preparedness movement was gaining strength in the States. As part of that, the women dressed in Mandarin costumes and served tea to the city's wealthy elite amidst a recreation of a Chinese tea garden. The goal was to raise money for the purchase of an aeroplane for the coastal defense of New York, New Jersey, and Connecticut.

The *Evening Sun* photograph that ran with the initial story about the crime showed Sarah, nineteen and brunette, in her full-length cheongsam, laughing and winking at the camera as she left the building. The hands of the court clock behind her were poised at nine minutes past two o'clock.

Based on the court clock in the photo and the estimated time to travel by taxicab to her apartment on West 23rd Street, New York City police detectives believed she returned from the charitable event about ten minutes to three. On entering, she apparently surprised a robber, was subdued after a struggle, and then kidnapped. The abductor fled with the girl in her own automobile, a Packard, which was eventually found abandoned in the swamplands by the Harlem River.

Two days after her disappearance, her family received the first ransom note. It was written in a childish, left-leaning script (that of a right-handed person writing left-handed, police believed), and it demanded $50,000 for her safe return.

The note included one final, haunting sentence penned by the girl.

"Papa, please pay him and hurry. *Sarah.*"

John Nolan

2

The Detective

❧

JUST BEFORE MIDNIGHT on the day after Christmas, John Nolan sat on a low hill above one of the largest estates in New Rochelle. Using binoculars, he was watching the barns and paddocks for telltale wisps of smoke in the bright moonlight. The house, the summer home of a shovel manufacturer who wintered in Florida, was closed for the season, save for the comings and goings of caretakers and cleaning women.

A private detective, Nolan had been assigned by his agency to monitor this and four other estates in Westchester County, north of Manhattan. The properties' owners had hired the agency based on the suspicion that the staffs were using the estates' outbuildings to brew liquor illegally. With the European war on, imports of alcohol from the continent were expensive, and unlicensed stills were cropping up in rural areas. Just days before, Connecticut state police raided a barn outside Hartford, finding a still and a dozen hogsheads of more than sixty gallons each, all containing liquid mash in various states of fermentation.

Nolan had been on the hill, a treeless rise on the edge of a pasture, for nearly four hours. Though he was wrapped in a woolen blanket, the snow was above his boots and the icy December wind, made worse by the open location and elevated landscape, was nearly unbearable.

Again, he glanced over his shoulder for Sean Tierney, the

owner of the detective agency that employed him. Nolan did not know how to operate an automobile, so each night Tierney would personally drive him the ten or so miles from the city up to Westchester County to assume his post near one of the houses. Tierney dropped him off at eight o'clock and retrieved him at midnight, having spent the intervening hours in a warm roadhouse dining room or tavern.

Sitting on a wooden packing crate, Nolan felt a sudden cramping in his calf. Instinctively, he shot out the leg but lost his balance and tumbled into the snow. He reached for the pasture fence to brace himself, and a nail head on the fence post raked his wrist. Cursing under his breath, he watched the scrape to see if blood would emerge from the torn skin. A small amount did, and he cursed under his breath. As he dabbed at it with a handkerchief, he was overcome with despair. It was not the blood; it was everything about his wretched life at that moment.

At twenty-seven years of age, he was just a year removed from Ellis Island and Ireland, and his fiancée depended on him to make enough money to bring her over from County Carlow. Nolan could not understand how life had brought him here—freezing to his bones in a place he could not possibly find on a map, in a country that was not his and might never feel that way.

Indeed, he felt his real life was somewhere in the future. His current existence was not part of it. Wake up in a cold tenement, wash, dress, eat, go to work, come home, eat, sleep. There was no enjoyment in any of it. It was merely a grueling means of reaching a better place.

Minutes later, shivering so much that he could not keep his binoculars steady, Nolan heard the approach of a machine on the road below the pasture. Seeing no headlamps—they were turned off so as not to alert any illegal brewers—he knew it was Tierney, who was soon mounting the hill.

"Anything?"

"Nothing," Nolan said, feeling the ache in his knees as he rose.

"Then let's go. I brought you coffee and rolls. Is this going to be dinner for you?"

"It'll have to be." Nolan took the tin canister and the bag of rolls and folded the blanket.

"I've got some news for you," Tierney said, picking up the crate. "The man whose summer place you watched Monday ... Gates? Well, he called me this morning. I once did some work for him in regards to his ex-wife. You must've read about a girl what was kidnapped in the city last week."

Nolan shook his head.

"The Dutton girl? The rich girl? The only girl the rags are bothering to write about."

"I guess I saw something."

"She's actually the Gates girl. He divorced the mother, who remarried a man named Dutton. But the girl is his own daughter. He wants us to take up the case."

"What can we do that the police can't?"

"Solve it. Find the girl before this kidnapper kills her," Tierney said, pulling his overcoat higher on his throat. "Now listen, dammit, you have to learn to drive. I can't stand making this trip every night. My God, it's freezing in that machine."

Nolan started to say, "You're not the one who has to sit out here," but he refrained. He knew just how Tierney would snap at him. "Be happy you've got any job, you Irish shit." Perhaps he should be happy, but fourteen dollars a week should not be enough to buy any employer such misery.

Instead, Nolan was diplomatic. "Maybe you shouldn't take jobs this far out of the city."

He got a sharp reaction anyway. "Dammit, if I don't get offered nothing else, this is what I'll take—unless you don't want to work. Do you? Well ... do you?"

"Yes, I want to work. Of course I want to work."

"Then quit complaining. I brought you coffee, didn't I?"

In silence, they began to descend the hill, following the path of already trampled snow. Gusts of wind exploded off the pasture, whistling by Nolan's ears, which were so numb by now that he could only hear the whipping wind but could not feel it.

Tierney was Nolan's older cousin on his mother's side. Well over six feet tall, he was broad in the shoulders and broader still in the waistline, the result of excessive beer and other starches. His shaving habits were deliberately irregular to keep a scruffy, mean appearance. That was "a necessary thing" for a detective, he would say. In the journey to America, Tierney had preceded his younger, smaller cousin—Nolan was a lean five feet nine—by a decade.

Tierney had been able to get a job on the New York City police force because his uncle was already a detective in the department when he arrived in 1905. However, he lost his job in 1913 during the graft and corruption scandals. It had come to light that owners of the city's "disorderly resorts"—hotels and rooming houses used by prostitutes—were paying fees to local police for protection from raids. Although forced to resign, Tierney was never charged. ("But I'll admit, that money bought me my motor and my house in Queens.")

Family tie or no, Nolan had mixed feelings for Tierney, who often treated his younger cousin with the kind of disdain a Mayflower Bradford might heap upon a newly arrived Irish immigrant. By virtue of a few years head start, Tierney seemed to feel he was entitled. Nolan did not agree.

There was some other element in Tierney's disdain, Nolan suspected: jealousy. Nolan was the kind of quiet, handsome, well-mannered young man that attractive single women, especially Irish women, admired. Tierney had never been that kind of man, explaining his subtle resentment of Nolan—and of better-looking women for their lack of interest in him.

With his fine features, black hair, and athletic build, Nolan had been mistaken several times during his year in New York for the popular stage actor George Kiefer. The comparisons made him curious enough that he went to a matinee of Kiefer's play, *The Forgotten Years*, at the Majestic Theatre. Personally, he saw only a slight resemblance, but he was stopped in the lobby as he left by a group of schoolgirls demanding autographs. When they refused to believe he was not the actor, he signed the man's name on their programs to escape them.

As they reached the Mitchell roadster, Tierney stopped and turned. "Now look, Cousin, day after tomorrow, Monday, we're meeting Gates then going to see the apartment where this daughter was grabbed. So, show respect for this tormented man."

"I would never say anything that—"

"What I'm saying is just shut up and let me talk," he said, opening the operator's door. "Let's go. You crank it. I'll spark it."

Captain Gates

3

The Crime Scene

༄

"**C**ALL ME 'CAPTAIN,' boys."

"Gates doesn't sound Irish, Captain," Tierney said.

"It isn't but I am," said Gates. "My father was Gates. From Liverpool. My mother was O'Toole. From Dublin."

Nolan and Tierney were following the rotund man up Sixth Avenue after meeting him outside a lunchroom at 17th Street. The other side of sixty, Gates had a thick, drooping mustache and thinning hair, and he wore a red carnation in the lapel of his greatcoat. They'd learned Gates had served in the New York State Militia, attaining the rank of captain before turning to other endeavors. He made his fortune buying and selling real estate around the city.

In the heart of the so-called "ladies' mile" along Sixth, where stores like Siegel-Cooper and O'Neill's Dry Goods sold fashion, foods, and furnishings, the lunchtime crowds of clerks and shop girls filled the sidewalk. Traffic was heavy on the avenue. A few years earlier, it would have been all horse-drawn wagons and carriages. Now it was nearly all automobiles, with blaring horns and smoking engines.

Indeed, progress had come with breathtaking speed since the turn of the century. Wireless telegraphy, automobiles, aeroplanes, motion pictures—they had all become commonplace in a matter of years. Before leaving Ireland, Nolan had never seen a building higher than four stories. In April, he stood on Broadway near City Hall at seven thirty one evening to watch the electric lights go on for the first time inside the Woolworth Building, the tallest building in the world at nearly sixty stories. President Wilson himself threw the switch from the White House to light the structure.

"Before we get there, let me just say something." Gates stopped on the sidewalk and turned to them, appearing to be holding back strong emotions. "What's happened to my daughter is the worst thing that's ever happened in my life, that could ever happen in any father's life. Once, years ago, I got robbed and beat up bad. I was in Brooklyn, coming out of a barber shop. You can always tolerate your own pain, boys. It's the suffering of someone else, someone you love, that hurts the most. The thought of him taking her and me not knowing whether she's dead or alive .... I ... I can't even talk about it."

He turned away and continued walking, his pace brisker than before.

"We're very sorry, sir," Nolan said.

"How long you boys been over here?" Gates asked.

"Myself, I've just been in these United States since oh-five," Tierney said. "Nolan, here, since a year ago. Also from Ireland."

"Ireland? Really? I couldn't tell, boys. Honestly, could your accents be any thicker?"

"Where's yours, Mr. Gates ... Captain? I don't hear nothing of the wonderful brogue," Tierney said.

Gates gave him a disapproving look as they strode along the sidewalk, maneuvering through the slower-moving pedestrians, many of whom were still eating egg sandwiches and sipping from tins of bean soup purchased from curbside peddlers. "What are you so proud of? Of being Irish?"

"Not at all, Captain," Tierney said. "I ain't ashamed of it neither."

Above 22nd Street, the crowds on the sidewalk thinned, and Gates picked up the pace again. Nolan could imagine his apprehension about going back into the apartment.

"Let me ask you," Gates said. "The Irish come to America, and what do they do? They live in a neighborhood that's all Irish already. They dress like the neighborhood, in those ugly billycock hats and trousers six inches off their shoes. They talk like the neighborhood, making too much of their Rs. And they go to apply for jobs wearing their Irish brogues like a suit of clothes, and when they don't get them, they wonder why. You should imitate the accents of these fellows in the investment offices on Broad Street. My mother never lost her Irish accent. I heard it all my life. But I chose to talk like my father and I've never been without employment." He stopped. "This is the building."

They reached an address off the avenue on West 23rd Street owned by Gates, an apartment house of beige sandstone.

"You fellows smell anything?" Gates asked as he was about to enter.

"Not me," Tierney said.

"Smells like a sewer," Gates said.

They went into the front hallway. Painters were preparing to refinish the wood floors, and unopened cans of lacquer were stacked along the wall. Gates stopped in front of the first apartment door, took out a long string of keys, and found the proper one. Unlocking the door, he walked inside and sniffed the air. "Don't you boys smell it? A stink?"

"Nothing really," Tierney said, as he and Nolan followed.

"The way you're going to find whoever kidnapped her," Gates said, "is he took things from this apartment, mainly jewelry. He was here to rob her, and he'll pawn these things eventually .... You don't smell anything? It's a smell like a sewer pit."

"Nothing, Captain." Tierney stayed right at Gates' shoulder.

Paintings. It was what first caught Nolan's eye when they walked into the parlor. What really separated the wealthy from the rest of us, he thought, were paintings on the walls.

"Everything is just how the police found it, boys. Nothing's been moved."

There were a few chairs and tables overturned on the large oriental rug that covered the wood floor. There were also small items, magazines and sofa pillows, scattered about the room, indicating a struggle. Otherwise, the furnishings were elegant.

Gates was wiping his eyes with a handkerchief.

"Is this your first time back, Captain?" Tierney asked.

Gates glared at him. "You think this is the first time I've set foot in here? Her own father? My God, you're supposed to be the detective."

"I meant first time since she got kidnapped."

"I mean the same thing! My God, man, when the police call you up and tell you your daughter's been taken, God, you rush right over!"

"I just … I was …" Tierney's voice trailed off.

"Sir, how valuable were the jewels he stole?" Nolan asked, attempting to change the subject.

"Well, there were three pieces—one a necklace of two hundred pearls with a diamond and sapphire clasp. Another's a bracelet of three separate strands of diamonds, and the other's a crescent brooch with particularly large diamonds. I've got photographs of all of 'em. They were on the books for … well, I don't want to tell you the exact amount, boys, but for many thousands of dollars. I will tell you one piece, the necklace, was thirty-seven thousand by itself."

"I hope there was insurance," Tierney said.

"There was, but not enough. I gave my daughters these things—I have a second daughter, by the way—I gave them these things because, well, like any father, I wanted them to have assets of their own. There was a divorce, you see, and legally … well, to make sure these assets didn't go into the hands of someone I didn't want to have them, I gave them as gifts to my daughters before the lawyers ever got into it. They were taken from a steamer trunk Sarah kept in her bedroom closet."

Tierney started to light his pipe but thought better of it. "Can I ask about this ransom note, Captain, the particulars of it?"

"Just what you'd expect. 'I have your daughter. I want money or else I'll kill her.' He said she came home while he was looking for her valuables and that was her bad luck. Then he had her sign the damn thing and write a little message. 'Papa, please pay him and hurry.' It was her signature. I'm certain of that. I cried when I read it. I feel no shame in saying it."

"What happened then? Did he call you?"

"At my office two days later. Detectives said the call came from a public phone in a saloon in the Bronx. But no one there remembers the man. He talked with a real screechy, high-pitched voice, clearly disguising it. He wanted the money right away, but I said I had to get a bank loan, that all my money was tied up in my properties. It was a lie, but he believed it. He calls every couple days from a different place and I tell him there's still paperwork. But I know this for certain. If I pay him, he'll kill her 'cuz she can identify him. And if I don't pay him, he'll kill her anyway."

"A hard situation, Captain."

"The people I've been talking to say to stall him as long as possible and hope all you detectives can find her first."

"Sir, if someone robs people, they need money," Nolan said. "So while he waits for the ransom, he might try to sell the jewels cheap. Are police checking the pawnshops?"

"You got your brain working, Mr. Nolan. Very good," Gates said. "If police are checking the pawnshops, I haven't heard anything about it. What's it been, eight days? So that's why I want you boys on this. The police in this city are incompetent. The criminals and the police—one's no better than the other. They all arrived on the same boat but got off on different gangplanks. Boys, never go on the force, if you can help it."

"I'll remember that, Captain," Tierney said, gesturing to Nolan to keep quiet. He picked up a silver candlestick from a side table. "This robber wasn't too bright. He missed this."

"He got the most expensive stuff," Gates said. "So he was bright enough."

"Maybe he was about to fill his bag with it when your daughter waltzed in and caught him at it," Tierney said without thinking. "Sorry, Captain. I shouldn't have said that."

Gates turned away, shaking his head.

Nolan, who had been quietly opening drawers and closets, had found several other items—an intricate, cut-crystal bowl, a silver salt cellar, and several silver-plated dishes—that any observant burglar should have taken.

He walked down the back hallway to the kitchen. The splintered alley door the robber had apparently entered had been hastily repaired with screws and scrap wood. Beside it, a replacement door leaned against the wall, still wrapped with tradesman's cloth.

A tiny, framed, handwritten card posted by the door caught his eye. "Mind thy kitchen and keep it clean. If six days of labor are not enough, thou couldst do worse than continue on the seventh."

He had to smile. Had Sarah written it herself? He looked around, picking up items. Sarah's plates and silverware. Sarah's apron. Sarah's soup kettle. In a bowl by the ice box were a half dozen potatoes, all sprouting roots. He shook his head at the poignancy of it. He thought about where she might be at that moment. Tied up and gagged in a dark warehouse maybe, her frantic, muffled screams unable to reach anyone's ears.

Nolan went to the alley window and peered out. A narrow brick service road, crowded with overflowing garbage cans, ran between the two rows of buildings. Above it, telephone and electric lines as well as wash lines—the laundry flying like flags—crossed haphazardly between the rows. Odd. Expensive apartments, and what lay behind them was just as ugly as what was behind his own desolate tenement.

He looked briefly into the bedroom. The steamer trunk, with its broken lock, was out of the closet. He looked about, opening drawers on her dresser and peering under the bed. He noticed that her silver jewelry box, containing her everyday rings, bracelets, and necklaces, was still atop the dresser. Why would the robber leave that?

When he returned to the living room, Gates, who was leafing through an album of family photographs, turned to him.

"Where'd you go, Mr. Nolan? Is it John?"

"Yes, sir."

"Please. It's Captain."

"Sorry, Captain."

"Well, you're the quiet lad, and I notice you're very observant, very keen. You've been out back and looked everywhere, I'm guessing."

"I'm just trying to absorb as much as possible. I might not get a second chance."

"Good boy."

Tierney bristled. "I've been absorbing it too, Captain, but I've been trained so you don't see me doing it."

Gates seemed to scoff—a quick rasping exhalation. "Sean, you keep at it then."

He asked Nolan what his ambitions were beyond detective work. Nolan said he was taking an evening course in bookkeeping at a public school near his apartment and saving his money.

"One day, I hope to work in the business field," he said.

"Exactly what I did," Gates said. "I took business courses at City College, saved my money, and lived on the cheap."

Gates turned to Tierney. "Sean, I want you to put John on the case full time. This kidnapper has to be found. I can't pay the bastard. I can't *not* pay him. And he has to be found quick. So what's it going to cost me ... if John is full time?"

"We'll talk about that privately, Captain."

Gates turned to Nolan. "What's he pay you?"

Tierney motioned to Nolan to keep quiet. "Captain, I don't want him getting into this."

"Sounds like it's not much."

Both Tierney and Gates looked at Nolan, expecting him to say something, but he remained silent, only smiling sheepishly.

Gates laughed. "Says it all. Tierney, make sure this boy gets most of what I'll end up paying you. Understand?"

"Yes, Captain. We'll work it out. Like I told you, I'll help where I can, but nearly all my boys is committed to two labor strikes right now."

As Gates began to wander away, Tierney smacked Nolan on the shoulder. Then Gates stopped and again sniffed the air. "By God, why is it I'm the only one who smells this stink."

"Captain, what did you have for lunch?" Nolan asked.

"Why, beer and cheese."

"Well, sir, I noticed you have bits of something in your mustache. It might be the cheese what you smell."

Gates brushed the mustache clean and a yellowish residue fell to the floor. "By God. You *are* a detective!"

New York Public Library

4

The Investigation Begins

∾↭

NOLAN SPENT THE afternoon at the New York Public Library, researching the kidnapping in the splendor of the vast main reading room, beneath the gilded ceiling and the massive globe chandeliers.

In a leather pocket diary used to record his expenses, he began a section devoted to the crime and the people around it. He drew from accounts of the kidnapping and the police investigation that he found in more than a dozen of the city's newspapers.

> One of the city's recent crop of debutantes, Sarah W. Dutton, was presented at the Grand Assembly at the St. Regis last spring. She was educated at the Peabody School for Girls in Hartford, Connecticut, receiving instruction in European art and interior decoration.
>
> Police determined that at the time of the kidnapping, only three people were in their apartments in Miss Dutton's 23rd Street building, and all said they heard nothing suspicious. The building contains mainly larger apartments, and many of the residents have the means to leave New York in winter for addresses in warmer climates.
>
> The crime was discovered by an express

package delivery man Sunday morning. On arriving at the address, he knocked on Miss Dutton's apartment door and received no response. As he was leaving the building, he glanced through the front window glass and saw conditions that suggested a robbery had taken place.

He immediately flagged a foot patrolman.

Miss Dutton's brother, Timothy P. Gates, has resided at several addresses in the city's Tenderloin district over the past three years, according to city records. He gives his occupation as artist. It is believed that Miss Dutton's sister, Julia Dutton, also resides in Manhattan, although the Dutton and Gates families would not confirm that information.

Mr. Robert T. Dutton, the victim's stepfather, was formerly the president of Van Wyck Cartage, Inc., a freight transport company that entered bankruptcy in September. Dutton was president of another transport company, Overton, Inc., that went bankrupt in 1909. He and his wife were in South America when the kidnapping took place and are reported to be making their way back.

BY FIVE O'CLOCK, exhausted by sitting and reading, Nolan left the library, resolving to walk as far uptown as he could for the exercise before catching a trolley home.

However, with cold winds whipping through the canyons of Fifth Avenue, he got only as far as St. Patrick's Cathedral on 51st Street. Having never seen the inside of the great gothic edifice, and hearing a pipe organ playing, he found an open door, went in, and took a seat in a back pew of the nearly empty sanctuary to warm himself. Golden light streamed through the high, stained-glass windows as the chancel organ played.

Nolan had no love for the Catholic church. His first memories of priests were of beatings in school, so he had formed a lifelong distrust of them. At the same time, he grudgingly recognized that the church had a place in his life.

Religion in his own life was simple. It was God's will that he come to America. And it was God's will that he marry Sheenagh Casey. He knew nothing more of God's will than that. It was manifest in the persistence with which he felt these two things.

In his daily life, he drew on his own instincts and conscience for what was right and wrong, not on any knowledge of the Bible or on the questionable advice of the priests in his life. And with no immediate family in New York to goad him to attend church, he had been to Sunday Mass infrequently since arriving—and not once in the past six months.

He first heard of America from his uncles, sitting with them in parlors and taverns in Ireland as they traded stories. Probably, he realized now, they had heard them when they were young and sitting with their uncles. He believed few had actually been to America.

"Jobs so plentiful you have a choice of a dozen .... Rose up from nothing to become .... No thought of being Catholic or Protestant or even Hindu. You're an American only ...."

He finally decided to go to America when his impoverished family was forced to move in the fall of 1913. His father had worked on and off as a traveling man for a sugar company. The home in which the Nolan family had lived for thirty years was leased, and the landlord, facing his own financial calamity, served writs of ejectment on all his properties in order to sell them. His parents moved to small rented rooms nearby. He bought a ticket to America.

In Nolan's year in New York, he had suffered as many deprivations as he ever had in Ireland. The reality of New York was far from the expectation of it. For weeks before he made the crossing, he and Sheenagh had written out plans and budgets and then alternate plans and budgets, should this or that go wrong.

Little had gone as expected. Jobs in America were fewer than promised—and more demeaning—and salaries were lower. The insults suffered for being Catholic and poor in Ireland were replaced by insults for being Irish and poor in the States.

Yet, stepping away from it all, he could see their goals were slowly being met. He was able to put some money in the bank each week, and they were closer to Sheenagh's arrival and their marriage each week.

Perhaps that was the dream of America. God placed in your

mind an exaggerated view of how good life there could be in order to convince you to want it and work for it. True, the reality would undoubtedly turn out to be less grand than expected. However—also true, he hoped—the reality would still be well worth the effort.

Warmed enough to feel a renewed resolve to reach home, he rose to leave but then sat back down in the pew. A realization had come over him. This kidnapping. He suddenly felt the importance of it in his life. The police were unable to solve it. The family was depending on him to solve it. And the poor girl might lose her life if he did not solve it. A challenge, was it not? A personal challenge. Should he save the girl and return her to her family, he might make the name he needed to succeed in America.

Although paid as a detective, he had not truly felt like one until that moment.

Police evidence photos

5

The Evidence

❦

TIERNEY ARRANGED FOR Nolan to view police photographs of the evidence and crime scene that were filed at the Second Branch Detective Bureau on 42nd Street, where Tierney had once been stationed.

"They won't let me in the building, so you gotta go. Ask for Billy Burgess and no one else. He knows you're coming and I already slipped him something, so you don't have to. And for God's sake, don't mention my name to anyone."

Nolan saved the taxi money Tierney gave him and walked the twenty blocks, suffering the snow flurries and icy winds. God, how he hated cold. In Ireland, it never seemed to be too hot or too cold, but here it never seemed to be anything else but too hot or too cold.

At the bureau, he entered through a two-story arch beneath the raised seal of the City of New York. He asked for Mr. Burgess and was directed to a large side office, which was unoccupied except for a small swarthy man in a rumpled gray suit who sat slumped at a typewriter.

He looked up. "You Tierney's man?"

"Yes, sir."

He stood and motioned Nolan to follow him. "All right, let's go, but shut up and don't mention Tierney's name. Just say you're a Pinkerton detective. Got it?"

They went down a hall and then up a back staircase.

"How long you worked in this business?"

"As a private detective? About three months."

"What's Sean got you doing?"

"Mainly serving subpoenas."

"Okay, when we go in, you just shut up." They came to a door—Evidence Repository. Inside, a man with his back to them was behind a counter like a bank teller's cage. Bars separated them.

"Clyde, this fellow needs to see some photographs in the Dutton case. The family hired him."

The clerk turned. He was lighting a cigar. "Does this fellow know we don't usually let outsiders look at the—"

"Don't bother. He's already paid for the privilege and I think there's something here for you." Burgess slid some coins across the counter. The clerk pocketed them quickly and went in the back to retrieve a folder. Then Burgess led Nolan to an empty interrogation room on the same floor.

"I'm going for a pipe, but I'll be back in fifteen minutes. Then I'll take you downstairs and you can read the detective's report. Remember, you're a Pinkerton man and you don't know Tierney. You got it?"

The small room, with its flaking white cement walls, smelled simultaneously of disinfectant and cigar smoke. There was an unpainted wooden table and three chairs at the center of it, with metal rings attached to the table edges for shackling prisoners being questioned.

Nolan took out his leather pocket diary to take notes. His heart began to race as he opened the folder of photographs and slid out the thick, glossy sheets. He moved to study them more closely under the bare overhead bulb.

The first was of the parlor. It was identical to what he had seen when he had visited the apartment with Mr. Gates. He was aware of the strange orderliness of the mess in the room.

Odd, he thought. The few chairs and tables that lay on the floor had been against a wall prior to the crime. In the photograph, they were turned over onto the carpet as if they had simply been pulled forward until they toppled. Had a life-and-death struggle actually produced this?

He tried putting himself in the mind of the robber. Clearly, money was his foremost concern. He broke in when she was not there, so he had been trying to avoid the very thing that had happened, a confrontation with her. Perhaps he was busily grabbing valuables when he heard her key in the front door lock, so he hid behind the sofa, as it was the largest thing in the parlor. She came in and saw that some cherished possession was missing. She walked about, investigating, suddenly discovered this man, and screamed. He grabbed her to silence her. They wrestled violently, arms flailing, chairs and tables flying about. Finally, she stopped resisting. He told her that if she moved again, he would kill her. Then, the struggle over, he would have looked for something he could use to tie her up and gag her.

Nolan stared at the sheet. How had the scenario he imagined resulted in this photo?

It could not.

Now he became aware of something else in the photo. As Tierney had observed, there were many valuables left untouched on the tables that were not upset. Candlesticks, silver bowls, porcelain figures. The kidnapper had wrestled the girl into submission and had the time to tie her up and bring the girl's Packard to the kitchen door and get her into it. Wouldn't he have had the time to come back and collect these valuables? After all, that was what he was really there for.

He went back to the folder and studied the other photographs. A detective proudly holding up a small sledgehammer for the camera. The broken lock on the apartment's back door where the robber entered. The empty garage bay where the girl's Packard had been stolen.

There was also a photo of the steamer trunk with its lock broken, where the jewels had been hidden. He closed his eyes and thought of the room as he had seen it. He had opened the dresser drawers and found nothing amiss. Like many women, Sarah carefully folded her clothes, forming perfect stacks and rows. There had not been a wrinkle in anything, and her silver jewelry box was still on the dresser.

Again, he put himself in the mind of the robber. He went into this room in search of valuables. He managed to find the jewels in the bottom of this steamer trunk, but would he not have looked first in the dresser drawers, shoving these things aside in his rushed and hasty search? Would he not have grabbed the jewelry box on the dresser to take with him?

Nolan was certain. This robber knew where the jewels were,

and he knew the value before he ever set foot in the apartment. He was there only for them.

Then there was a photo of the ransom note, written in a childish hand. Police believed the writer was right-handed and had chosen to write it left-handed to disguise himself.

> Dear Mr. Gates,
>
> I have your daughter. Do not follow my directions and it will go bad for you and very bad for her. Just do what I say and she will be freed. I want $50,000. I will contact you soon by calling your office from a place far from where she is, I promise you.
>
> I did not plan to kidnap your daughter. She came home when I was looking for valuables in her apartment so it was her unfortunate luck.
>
> To prove I have your daughter, I will have her write something below:
>
> Papa, please pay him and hurry. *Sarah*

There was also a photograph of a close-up of her signature. The S in it had a distinctive flourish.

The last photograph was a shot of a large, framed oil painting of Sarah, a studio portrait. Perhaps it had been photographed as identification. It showed her standing on a hill in spring or summer, wearing a long, white dress and carrying a parasol over her shoulder. He had noticed it mounted on the dining room wall at the apartment, but at the time he had not studied it.

Nolan imagined the stretch of days during which the portrait was painted. Perhaps it was spring in New York. For her, the world had been hopeful, the dogwoods in Central Park in bloom, everything good in life ahead.

Nolan had no brothers, but he had four older sisters, and when he was seven, the oldest, Siobhan, disappeared in Manchester, England. Just sixteen, she had been excited about finding a place for the summer as a nanny in the home of a barrister. Weeks after arriving in the city, she did not return from the green grocers one morning. A month-long search by police failed to find any evidence of her. Two years later, a skeleton with only gray shreds of flesh remaining on it had been discovered in a forest outside the city. A female, age sixteen to twenty in the medical examiner's estimation. No clothes or other possessions had been found at the scene to fix the identity—apparently the precautions of a careful abductor. However, Nolan's father, who went to claim the remains, was sure it was her.

Nolan had only a vague memory of his oldest sister, but looking at this painting of Sarah in the photo, he could not help but see her in Sarah's face. The confidence. The restrained excitement at life's prospects. The thrill she must have felt to find herself a young, pretty girl in a bustling city. Had it been this same smiling expression that had turned to horror at the startling appearance of the robber?

He winced with pain at the thought of where Sarah might be at that moment. She might be suffering, convinced she would never see her family again, certain she would die. He stared at the painting in the photo. It haunted him, knowing the end that would soon arrive for her if he did not succeed in finding her.

Sean Tierney

6

The Agency

~∾

"**S**O WHAT? So the furniture didn't fit your particular idea of what a wrestling match should do to it," Tierney said. "How many times have you wrecked a room in a fight?"

"What I'm saying is—"

"Cousin, there's no single way a room should look. You weren't there. So you have no idea how it played out."

Nolan stood and moved his chair against the wall. They were in the cramped office of the Tierney Detective Agency on the city's West Side, a block off the Hudson River. Three chairs, a desk, a safe, and a stove. In winter, one smelled only the coal heat from the stove. In summer, the rancid smell from floating garbage in the river was the principal odor.

"Now, imagine," Nolan said. "I knock into this chair from this direction. It falls like this. From this direction, it falls like that. Think of some way I could hit this and it falls straight forward from the wall like this. You can't. Yet every piece of furniture in that front room fell straight forward onto the floor. It doesn't make sense is what I'm saying."

Tierney took a tobacco pouch from his vest pocket and filled his briar pipe. As he patiently tamped it, he studied his cousin. "Well then, Nolan. Tell me. What's your great theory of the case?"

"I don't have a theory. Right now, I just have these questions." He returned to his leather diary.

"Then here's my theory." Tierney lit the pipe by striking

a match on the desk. "And it's the theory of the police also, from what you tell me. This robber, he gets himself inside the apartment. He's going about filling his bag, he makes an intelligent guess and finds the hidden jewels, but then he hears her key—"

"It wasn't no intelligent guess, Sean. He—"

"Let me finish. So he hears her key in the front door. What does he do? He drops down behind the sofa and hides, thinking he'll kill her if she sees him. Then your man here, he decides no, this rich girl is better to him for ransom than dead. So even if she saw him, which I'm sure she did, he didn't kill her right off. He grabbed her, they fought, the furniture toppled, he got control of her, maybe tied her up. Then he got her out of there, wrote his ransom note, had her sign it, and he killed her. What's he need her alive for after that? She'd be able to identify him. She's probably in her grave out in the woods somewhere."

Nolan sat now and thought a second. "Go back to this idea of how he found the jewels, what you say is an intelligent guess. I don't think—"

"Cousin, robbers know where people hide their valuables. It's what they teach you first day in robber's school. He made a very smart guess they was in that trunk."

"I don't think so. I think someone was in on it with him. They knew where those jewels were and how valuable they were."

Tierney eyed him as if challenging him. "Then let's hear your evidence."

Nolan, agitated, rose and began to pace the small office floor. "A robber breaks into a place—he would grab the expensive things he could see right out in the open because he would want to get out as quick as possible. But this robber passes up silver things in that parlor worth hundreds. And that steamer trunk, it was hidden away in the bottom of a closet in a back bedroom. It's not like it was out in the open. Even the most intelligent guess ever would not lead him there. He knew where they were, and he knew how valuable they were—to pass up all that silver and such."

"Maybe."

"And that bedroom shows no sign he looked anywhere else but in that steamer trunk. No clothes from the dresser scattered around, no storage boxes pulled out from under the bed and opened up. I'm absolutely certain someone who knew where the jewelry was put this thief up to it."

Tierney shook his head so the smoke from the pipe created a twisting snake of gray in the air. "I don't say I disagree, but I don't say I agree either."

"And this fight you say they had—I don't believe it," Nolan went on. "It looks like there was no fight at all, like the room was made to look like there was a fight."

Tierney bridled at being contradicted. "Nolan, you look at some photos and you know *all* about it, even though you've never spent a day doing police work. The obvious truth *is* the truth—that's what I've learned from years doing this. Besides, the girl is still kidnapped. And whether he knew where these jewels was or not, whether the fight was a fight or not, it doesn't change nothing. The girl still has to be found."

They were silent for a moment.

"Anything else?" Tierney said.

Nolan sat and turned his eyes back to the diary. "The detectives that Sunday who investigated the apartment. Keyes and Cochran. How reliable are they?"

Now three men walked into the office, one of Tierney's detective squads. They were all former policemen, big men in long overcoats. They deposited black billy clubs on the desk.

"We were told to not bring these no more."

"It's a union strike," Tierney said. "What do the bosses want you to bring?"

"Shotguns."

"I don't have any shotguns here," Tierney said.

"Then bigger revolvers. The Colts. The long barrels."

Tierney sighed. "I'll have to get them from home. Take the Smith and Wessons today. Tell them you'll have the Colts tomorrow."

Tierney went to the safe to withdraw the Smith & Wessons.

Nolan could ride the trolleys and walk the streets of the city and often be the tallest person in sight, especially in immigrant neighborhoods. However, in any group of policemen or detectives, he was usually the smallest. Those were people hired for their size—imposing men, physically able to get their way when they had to.

One of the men glanced at Nolan then turned away dismissively. Tierney's harmless cousin. Nolan liked to perpetuate that particular view of himself, especially before Tierney's detectives. The small, harmless cousin.

Much of the private detective work in the city had to do with infiltrating unions and fighting union strikers, but Nolan sympathized with the unions, not the bosses. When the city's paperhangers and painters went out on strike over wages, Tierney sent him to attend a strike rally to report who spoke. He liked what he heard and instead claimed he wrote down the address wrong and missed the rally.

Nolan led Tierney to believe he knew little about defending himself, which meant the assignments he got—serving legal papers, guarding houses, keeping the agency's books—were not likely to lead to violence, which he very much wanted to avoid. He did not intend to stay a detective and thought it a poor and dangerous way to make a living.

However, growing up in an Irish village where trouble was the antidote to boredom, Nolan had been in numerous fights. Not because he started them. Small for his age when he was very young, he was frequently the target of larger boys.

What he learned from those scraps was this: Fight dirty and fight with a frenzy. Pummel any boy who would attack you with three punches for every one he threw. Jump on him. Kick him. Bite him if necessary. Make him remember the experience the way an animal remembers its tangle with a badger. It was something it never wanted to repeat. Eventually, when he reached five feet nine, those petty fights ended, but something else began. Fights with weapons.

When he was sixteen, he was slashed with a pair of small sewing scissors, hidden until the moment they appeared in the hand of his attacker, during a fight at an agricultural fair. So he had to reconsider his strategy.

He found a plumber's brass pipe collar in an uncle's workshop. It looked like a thick wedding ring, large and rounded in its outer side and flat on the inner side. He was left-handed and began to wear it as a ring on his right hand, and if needed, he could subtly transfer it to the middle finger on his left hand, his punching hand. The first time he employed it was later that year. A tramp, inches taller and many pounds heavier, tried to steal his packages as he waited behind a railway station in Muine Bheag, Ireland. One punch and the fight was ended. The brass ring landed on the man's mouth, deeply splitting his lip and probably dislodging teeth.

He brought the ring with him to New York and never let it out of his right hand—unless it had to be moved to his left. There were times, though, when he wore it on his left hand as a wedding ring to discourage women's interest.

The squad of detectives, armed with revolvers, left. Tierney, relighting his pipe, turned back to Nolan. "What were we talking about?"

"Keyes and Cochran. They were the detectives that Sunday. Are they reliable?"

"Never heard of 'em. But think about Sunday." Tierney leaned back and puffed his pipe, the abundant smoke from it filling the small office. "Your regular boys—the experienced boys—they aren't working Sunday. So who do the captains get for the Lord's day? Why, the worst of the worst. They're just trying to wrap up every case as quick as possible and get back to their cigars and nickel beers. Arrest anyone what's poor, manufacture some evidence, make 'em confess. Case over and done. Yes, sir."

Nolan had to laugh, as much as he did not like encouraging Tierney. Given any provocation, his cousin would launch into a rant or rage, with the poor immigrant often the target. Irish, Italian, Russian—it did not matter.

Tierney leaned his chair against the plaster wall, apparently amused with himself. "Read off some more of the evidence, why don't you. I'll tell you what bits you can trust."

Nolan turned back to the diary. "Here. The police interviewed Sarah Dutton's fiancé. Colin Flannery. Apparently, they—"

"Good Irish boy, huh."

"They were engaged. He worked on the docks—a stevedore—for the Metropolitan Steamship Company until six o'clock. He was supposed to meet her at Proctor's Theatre just up the street from her apartment for a vaudeville show. She didn't show up, so he bought a ticket and went in himself. The detectives checked his employer. Yes, Flannery was at work till six. And Flannery gave them the program and the ticket stub, which he'd kept."

"What else?"

"There's a cook who works in a residence the other side of the service alley."

"Out back."

"Yes, an Italian woman who cooks and cleans for a banker. They interviewed her. She saw the robber going in Saturday afternoon. While she was in the kitchen washing dishes at the sink in front of a window that looks out on the alley, she saw a man enter Sarah Dutton's apartment through the service door. She glanced up and saw him enter. The door was already open by that time, but she saw the sledgehammer in his hand. She was very certain of the clock—twenty minutes before three—because she feeds the banker's terriers every day at exactly a quarter to three. She turned off the water and looked up while she dried her hands."

Tierney, working his pipe, nodded thoughtfully. "The thing about evidence like that, other detectives can go back and talk to the cook, they can talk to the fiancé, so that's not the kind of thing a Sunday detective would make up. He could get caught in a lie."

"She—the cook—saw the man clearly," Nolan said. "Five feet six, blond or light-brown hair under his cap, forty possibly. She said he looked Swedish. She never saw him come out because she went to clean in another part of the banker's apartment. But police found a second woman, a maid across the alley, who also thinks she saw the man walking in the alley Saturday afternoon. And she gave the same general description and the same time, about two thirty, without knowing what the cook said. Maybe five feet eight, she said. A soft cap, blond hair, carrying something like a hammer in his hand."

"What's the fiancé look like?"

Nolan flipped back through the pages. "Colin Flannery. Six feet, red hair, twenty-five possibly. He was at work anyway at three in the afternoon." Nolan put down the diary. "I still think the most important thing is how this thief found these jewels. I'm sure someone told him where they were. And if I can figure that out—who told him, who was in this with him—then I have a chance of finding the girl."

"Cousin, believe me, if there's any chance to save this girl's life, it's gonna be those jewels. They're gonna show up in a pawnshop or somewhere else real soon. And when they do, you've got your kidnapper. Concentrate on that and you got your *best* chance of finding this girl. Follow the jewels, Cousin." He paused. "Anything else?"

Nolan searched the diary. "That's it, I guess." He rose to put on his greatcoat.

Tierney, who had pulled out his tobacco pouch and was refreshing his pipe, idly studied Nolan as he buttoned his coat.

"You know," he said. "Your theories could actually work in our favor. If Gates thinks it ain't just this kidnapper working alone, like the police think, sure, that's good for us. He pays us to keep examining the whole situation. If this union strike ends, I can put more men on this. So go ahead, Nolan. You continue to puzzle it out—what this kidnapper thought, who he might be working with. Then we'll go to Gates. 'It might not be what the police believe, Captain. I want to put more men on it.'"

He puffed the pipe, pleased with himself. "Yes, by God. We've got alternative theories of the case, Captain, theories that need some serious exploration."

A photograph of Sheenagh

7

A Letter Home

~✺~

THE BEST PIECE of advice Nolan received about where to live in New York City came days before he left Ireland in January 1914.

"Stay out of Hell's Kitchen," a priest with a cork leg, who had lived in the city, told him. "The gangs there give no thought to maiming a priest, so how're they going to treat you, my son?"

When the Great Famine began in the 1840s, droves of Irish fled their homeland for America. Hell's Kitchen, on the West Side below 59th Street, and Five Points, in lower Manhattan, became the Irish strongholds in the city, attracting Irish gangs and crime.

Intent on avoiding trouble, Nolan found rooms uptown in a derelict tenement on 106th Street that housed a variety of impoverished immigrants. He took a fourth-floor, three-room apartment with a cylinder coal stove but no sink in the kitchen and a monthly rent of thirteen dollars. The cockroaches, mice, and rats came at no charge. A cold-water spigot and a single bathroom in the hallway served the entire floor.

To save money—and that was his goal above all else—he rented out one room. The current occupant was a French cabinetmaker who knew just enough English for the two to get along.

It was nearing midnight, and with his roommate asleep, he set a gas lamp at the kitchen table and prepared to write to his fiancée. First, he took out the small framed photograph that brought Sheenagh to mind more than any other. She'd been sixteen. It was taken as she posed in her Sunday dress in front of their family cottage prior to attending her cousin's confirmation. That summer, she had gone from a girl in whom one still saw hints of the child to a girl in whom one saw only the beautiful, grown woman. With brown eyes, dark-brown hair, and a graceful figure, she stood out in any crowd.

He first met Sheenagh in grammar school. Although she was four years younger, they shared a birthday, April sixth. In their rural school, where several grades of boys and girls were taught together, children with birthdays wore paper crowns throughout the day. He and Sheenagh would look across the classroom at each other when their day arrived, king and queen. With no words spoken, they formed a bond that grew into something deeper and undeniable over time.

He reread her most recent letter. Because their letters were delivered across the Atlantic by steamship, they were up to two weeks apart in their responses.

Dec. 16, 1914

My dearest John,

You will observe the postmark. Yes, I've moved to Dublin & am living with Michael, Aileen & their three children & have got a new job at the dockyard for war stuff. We are making floating targets to train the military gun crews. Aileen is convalescing from the grippe & Thomas, the 1 yr old, is producing a new tooth every day. We are making many decorations for Christmas.

I am hearing people are growing afraid of going to America because of German submarines in the Atlantic. I have to come soon, lest I lose my courage. I've saved about 21 £. What is that in American dollars? How do you stand in your savings? Should we lower our savings goal?

How is Sean treating you? Does he make you carry a pistol? —altho I hope not.

I worry about you so much. I hear stories about Irish girls going to America & forgetting they are Irish girls & losing their manners & propriety. I fear that this Irish girl will lose out in the competition with them, especially if we are separated much longer.

Please continue to write. If I miss a letter, I fret about what that means in regards to your safety & your feeling for me. And please please keep the habit of attending Mass, John. Please.

Forever your Sheenagh

She perfumed her writing paper for him. He lifted the letter to his nose and closed his eyes, savoring the lavender. Then he set out a fresh piece of paper, picked up a fountain pen, and began.

December 29, 1914

Dearest Sheenagh,

I'm resolved from now on to write you two letters every week, not only to assure you that every few days will bring a letter to you but also because my own loneliness for you grows every day. Even writing words on a paper to you feels like you're here in the room and I'm talking to you.

The last letter of yours is of Dec. 16. I'm sure others are on the way. Please give a kind greeting to Michael and Aileen and I hope your Christmas was wonderful. Mine did not exist because I had to work and because you were not here.

In regards to finances I have saved 304 American dollars in the bank and with your savings we have about 390 dollars American money. Our goal was 500 but I feel 400 will be able to start us on life here with what I know about expenses now. I checked with Royal English Lines and the latest ticket price out of Liverpool would be about 55 dollars— about 12 £—for second class to New York. I came steerage but I don't want you to have that terrible experience. So plan on February or March when the passage weather might be a bit better and you can go out on deck.

As for the Germans—so far their target is the British and not Ireland or America. The talk in America is to stay out of the war as long as possible and the Germans want to encourage that I'm sure. So hopefully the passenger ships coming here will not be bothered.

Tell my mother Sean is treating me well. To your question—No I don't carry a revolver and refuse to. Sean keeps trying to push one on me but I agree with you, I'm more likely to be shot if I'm carrying one myself. It works another way also. Sean mainly sends me out for the easy things like delivering subpoenas where a revolver isn't needed.

However he has me now on a case of a girl who was kidnapped from her apartment before Christmas. The police can't find her or figure out who is responsible and the poor girl's family has hired me. The police are cocksure the girl came in on a man who was there only to rob her valuables and he kidnapped her because it was another method to obtain money. But I believe more is going on than what meets the eye although I don't know what yet.

The police detectives are not the most brilliant men and they don't have a lot of reason to get to the bottom of it—it being easier to do nothing than to do something. But I like the challenge of the thing. It's my first real detective case on my own.

It rained the last two days instead of snow, so I bought an oilskin to throw over my greatcoat. I sincerely hope the buying of things is over and I can bank all what is extra of my salary each week.

My study of accounting is going well and I've passed the first and second exams. I go to classes one night a week at a public high school five blocks from my flat. My teacher is a man who teaches college accounting. He promises me there will be a job waiting when I finish in time for your arrival.

Lastly, do not even think about other women here in New York as I don't think about them and think only of you. We will be married the moment you arrive I promise. I wish for nothing more in life than that.

I will write again tomorrow and miss you terribly and yearn for your sweet kiss and gentle touch. And I will make a mighty effort to attend Mass I promise.

Forever your John

Police reserves outside the church

8

Church and Family

~~

SPECIAL MASS FOR
SARAH WILLINGHAM DUTTON

Archbishop authorizes prayers

Exclusive to the Evening World

A special Mass for Sarah Willingham Dutton, the young society woman believed kidnapped from her Manhattan apartment a week before Christmas, will be held tomorrow at the Church of St. Paul the Apostle on Columbus Avenue at 9:30 a.m., open only to invited family and friends.

Nevertheless, crowds of the curious are expected at the church, and police reserves from the 68th St. Station will be called out to maintain order.

Special prayers have been authorized by the Archbishop of the Roman Catholic Diocese of New York, Cardinal Farley.

Miss Dutton is the daughter of Arthur G.D. Gates, a prominent figure in the city's real estate field, who said yesterday that he has high expectations he will soon be reunited with his beloved daughter.

It is believed the girl's mother will attend, having returned from an excursion to South America.

* * *

HIS INVITATION IN hand, Nolan stood on the bottom steps of the church waiting for Tierney as light snow flurries fell on the city. On Columbus Avenue, horse-drawn carriages mixed with motors as they waited in line to unload their occupants. The steam from the horses' nostrils and the machines' engines rose quickly in the frigid air.

On the sidewalk, the uninvited shivered behind a line of policemen who were busy checking the invitations of those who desired to pass through.

Suddenly a horse reared, and its hind shoes lost traction on the ice-covered asphalt, tipping the animal precariously and causing the carriage to come up off its wheels on one side. With the clatter, everyone turned to watch. For a moment, there was no certainty as to how it would end, with the animal struggling to keep its balance. Ultimately it managed to stay upright, and the carriage fell back onto all its wheels.

This was the first time in New York that Nolan had occasion to wear his best suit, the only proper one he owned. Studying the wealthy friends of the Gates family as they passed, he did not feel so out of place as he would have thought. Nevertheless, out of place he was. Tierney had warned him, "Doesn't matter how well you dress, you won't be able to rub off the Irish."

He spotted Tierney. Other than his overcoat, his cousin wore his usual black bowler and wrinkled black wool suit. He had been forced to produce his invitation at the police line before being let through.

"Don't you look like something," Tierney said as he approached.

"Well, it is a Mass."

"You don't expect you're going in there, do you? Cousin, we're only hired to stand out here as guards."

"I thought the invitation—"

"It's just to get us right here, up on the steps. So, do your job."

When the snow grew heavier, the crowd, aside from the

police reserves, began to thin, so Tierney motioned that they could safely move up beneath the church's partially sheltered doorway, out of the weather. Nolan could vaguely hear the Mass inside, the funeral march, the tributes, and recitations. When Gates spoke, he heard only splintered phrases. "A joy to any father," "cruelly taken from the bosom of her family," "God's grace."

Soon the massive oak doors opened with a creak, and he and Tierney took their positions farther down the steps once again. Gates and his family were the first out, forming a receiving line. They were soon shaking hands with those who followed.

"Which one is the Dutton girl's mother?" Nolan asked.

"See Gates? Two down from him. Before the divorce, he had me follow her for a coupla weeks to try to catch her in something. I hear they hate each other now. Next to her is the man she married, Dutton. I heard his company has gone into bankruptcy. The wife's got all the money and pays all his bills. The fool."

"Who's the girl between the wife and Gates?"

"It's their older daughter, Julia. Quite a good-looking girl. But don't try talking to her. Gates will forbid it."

Nolan started to ask why, but could guess. Why put her through the misery of talking about her sister's kidnapping? Nolan watched her closely. She had on a somber black dress, elegant enough to pass for the kind of high fashion featured in magazines.

At one point, she lifted the veil on her broad hat to push loose strands of hair out of her vision and he was able to see her face. Certainly a striking girl.

"Now that last fellow, the one what walked up to Gates just now. That's the son. To Gates, he's a disgrace. An artist. He lives in the Tenderloin."

"I guess I should talk to him."

"He was in Albany the week the girl was kidnapped. His doctors verified it. He's been committed to asylums several times for his cocaine and alcohol habits. That's where he was. A farm. Albany police detectives did the work of checking it. The family couldn't even reach the boy to give him the bad news. No telephones."

"What's his name?"

"Timothy Gates. He kept the Gates name. The sisters didn't. They were angry as hell at their father for leaving their mother, so they took the Dutton name. But even though the son calls himself Gates, the captain won't talk to him. Watch. See if Gates even turns to greet him. Look how young Gates constantly glances at his father, waiting for him to turn. Gates can feel it, that glance on his back. He won't even acknowledge the boy."

True enough, Gates never turned to face the son, who finally walked away.

Tierney smiled at his own prescient observation. "Was I right?"

The snow flurries had halted, but the icy wind had quickened, causing the dusting of snow on the pavement to swirl in airborne eddies. As people moved down the stairs toward waiting transportation, Nolan managed a solemn expression to meet the eye of anyone who looked his way. As the line finished, Tierney moved up the steps toward Gates. Nolan followed.

"Captain, I just wanted to say how sorry we are," Tierney said.

Gates' daughter turned and fixed her gaze on Nolan, who removed his hat respectfully. She smiled at him and he returned it, something Tierney did not miss.

"Boys, talk to me tomorrow .... No. Actually, Nolan, you wait a second."

Gates spoke privately to his daughter, who walked down to the avenue where the taxis waited. Then he spoke to Tierney as if Nolan were not standing just feet away.

"One of the rag-bag newspapers got up another story about Sarah this morning, and by God, it printed my other daughter's address. Damn them." He glanced at her as she stepped into her taxi. "So this is what I want you to do. Post Nolan outside her building for a few nights. He isn't to talk to her or go inside. Just have him park outside and watch for anything."

Tierney seemed to revel in the idea Nolan was being ignored and he was not.

"Just give me the address, Captain, and Nolan will be there."

"I want him to park across the street and just sit in his machine."

"Captain," Tierney said. "Nolan doesn't know how to operate a motor. I could—"

He turned to Nolan. "Learn to drive, for God's sake!"

"I will, sir. Sorry."

"I could guard Julia, Captain," Tierney said. "I have a machine and—"

"No, I want John there. Look. I own the building. I'll have the building manager, who lives in the basement, I'll have him put out a chair for you in the first-floor hallway and let you in at six p.m. You stay there. Stay in that chair. My daughter has the second-floor, front apartment. Understand?"

"Yes, sir, Captain."

"And it's New Year's Eve tonight. She's not to go out and don't let anyone go in. Understand?"

Nolan nodded, took out his pocket diary, and recorded the address Gates provided. However, as he finished writing, out of the corner of his eye he saw a man rapidly approaching Gates from behind. Instinctively, he put himself between them, blocking his path. The man, about twenty-five, red hair, a scowling look, tried to shove Nolan out of the way, but Nolan held his ground.

Gates turned at the sudden commotion. "What do you want, Flannery?"

"Captain, I've called you twice but you—"

"I haven't taken the calls. What does that tell you?"

Flannery stepped around Nolan now, removing his bowler as he approached Gates to within a few steps.

"Captain, I had to read about this Mass today in the newspapers."

"It was only for family and friends."

Flannery sighed. "Captain, you know Sarah has feelings for me, strong feelings. She wants to get married. Don't you think you could take the time to find out who I am? Don't you think you could at least wonder if maybe I'm not, well, if maybe I'm not who you think I am?"

"Who are you, then?" Gates glared at him.

"Well, I'm not what you think I am. I know that. Sarah knows that. But this is why I want to talk to you. Sir, I'm hoping I can help find her, that I can help the police."

"Just tell the police what you know and then stay out of the way," Gates said.

"I already spoke to them. I told them everything I could think of. But I feel I can do more."

Gates smirked and turned away. "You should have done more before any of this happened. Then it never would've happened in the first place."

Portrait in oil of Julia Dutton

9

Guard Duty

~⌁~

A T DUSK, AS revelers were already beginning to crowd the streets of Manhattan, Nolan stepped off a trolley and began walking down East 52nd Street, looking for the number scrawled in his diary.

Despite this being a wealthy neighborhood—the Vanderbilts had once lived on the same street—the sidewalks were treacherous. A rain that morning had filled the boot prints in the trodden snow and then turned to ice as temperatures dropped in the afternoon. Nolan kept to the deeper snow for footing.

He finally saw the number, and through the window of the front door, he saw the building manager waiting for him, smoking a cigar.

"You the man Captain Gates sent?"

"Yes, sir."

"Here's your chair. Don't walk off with it." He disappeared through a door that led to the basement, shutting it behind him.

Nolan sat and surveyed the hallway. There appeared to be only one other apartment on the floor. He shook his head. His own tenement had six apartments to a floor.

A narrow Oriental carpet ran the length of the hallway atop varnished oak flooring. The walls were not painted; they were papered with a bright-gold, flowered pattern. A half-dozen electric sconces with etched glass shields lined the hallway—

and all were operating. His tenement had one hallway light that seemed to never work. Certainly no carpets.

He had been sitting nearly an hour when a woman leaned over the railing on the second-floor landing. She held a handkerchief.

"Excuse me. Are you here for me?"

Nolan stood and removed his hat. "I ... uh .... Are you Julia Gates?"

"Dutton."

"Sorry. Dutton."

"I am. And who are you?"

"Your father sent me. I'm John Nolan."

She did not say anything for a moment, just watching him. Her eyes, he could see now, were reddened.

"How do you expect to guard me if you're down there and I'm up here?"

"I ... your father ...."

"Why don't you pick up your chair and bring it up here, Mr. Nolan."

"But your father—"

"There's another hallway up here just as nice as the one down there. I just spoke to my father. He told me why you're here, even though I don't see any reason."

She retreated from the railing and Nolan did as told. As he reached the second-floor landing, he saw her apartment door close and then heard it lock.

Positioning the cane chair by her door, he settled in. Gradually, he became aware of gramophone music coming from inside her apartment. Opera, possibly. Then he heard what sounded like sobbing.

Poor girl, he thought. *Rich, but poor.*

Soon he could hear nothing but the gramophone. He realized there was never a time in his tenement that he heard nothing but music. The only noises he recalled were slamming doors, crying babies, arguments, and fights. Had he ever heard music in that building?

Now the door opened.

"Mr. Nolan, I forgot to ask. Have you had dinner?"

"Just what I had before I started."

"Which was what?"

"Some bread and cabbage."

She went away from the door, and in a few minutes, it swung wide and she appeared, carrying silverware and a plate of steak and potatoes.

"These are leftovers."

"Thank you, ma'am. Thank you very much."

He took it and she watched him sit in the narrow chair trying to balance the plate on his lap as he awkwardly took a bite.

"That isn't up to it," she said. "Why don't you come inside."

The apartment was warm, owing to a crackling blaze in the fireplace. Not since Ireland had he seen a wood fire indoors. It smelled so wonderful. In America, the poor mainly burned coal, which produced almost no flame, a sulfurous smell, and messy soot.

As in her sister's apartment, the fineness of the furnishings intimidated him. He might have taken the room for an exhibit in a museum, had he been told it was a display of the finest American domestic crafts. The tables were not just tables. They were sculpted art with inlaid patterns of ivory or exotic wood. The lamps were not just lamps. The shades had beadwork threaded through them, and the bases were inset with jewels. On all the walls, framed paintings were displayed, and the furniture surfaces were covered with small pieces—statuettes, glassware, silver trays, and pewter dishes.

Near the fireplace was the central piece of the room, a nearly life-sized portrait of Julia. It was leaning against a wall, perhaps too heavy to hang. Clearly, it was done by the same artist who painted the portrait of her sister that was in Sarah's apartment. Julia wore a long white dress, all linen and lace, and held a wide-brimmed "derby hat," as it was called in Ireland. The face was striking in its youthful, innocent beauty.

"If you want to know," she said, "what you're eating is sirloin steak and potatoes au gratin. My father wouldn't let me go out tonight, so this was my celebration."

"Au gratin. That's cheese, isn't it. It's very good."

"You don't look like a policeman. They're all ... well, much heavier than you, to be honest. But I guess on bread and cabbage, it's hard to get that way."

"I'm not a policeman. I'm a private detective."

"I didn't know there was a difference. You mean you don't work for the police department?"

"No, ma'am. Some detectives are in private service."

"Well, I've learned something."

She sat and silently watched him. Aware that he knew nothing of how people in society ate their food, he grew more awkward.

Suddenly she began to sob, taking a handkerchief from her sleeve.

"Excuse me," she said. "I can't control it."

"It's been a terrible experience, I'm sure."

"She almost never leaves my mind. When she does, I think of something that reminds me of her and straightaway, the crying." She took a deep breath. "So, you're trying to solve the case, are you. What have you found out so far?"

"Not much," he said, relieved that the focus was not entirely on his eating. "To be honest, the clues point in other directions than where the police detectives seem to think they point."

"What direction?"

"Well, the photographs ... and I apologize if I say anything to upset you."

"Please, I want to know."

"In the photographs, I don't see the things you would see if the crime happened in the way the police say it did."

"What do the police think?"

"That your unfortunate sister came home to interrupt a robber and, well, he decided to kidnap her."

"Aren't there other possibilities? Did anyone actually see a robber?"

"Yes, someone did."

"Someone saw him? I hadn't heard this," she said, moving forward on her chair now.

"Two women saw him, or at least who they think was the robber, in the back alley. One saw him at your sister's door."

"What did he look like?"

"He was less than my height and he wore a soft cap. He might have been about forty, maybe from Sweden or Finland or some such place. He had blond hair, they both said."

"Of course, a lot of men look like that," she said. "Maybe these women got the door wrong or the time wrong. Aren't there any other theories on how it happened? Aren't detectives supposed to examine all the theories?"

Nolan put the food aside and took out his diary and his Waterman pen. "In fact, I have my own theory. I believe someone hired this man to steal the jewels, someone who knew where they were. But then your sister arrived home early and the rest of it happened. Do you mind if I ask you some questions? It would help a great deal."

"I don't mind."

"When was the last time you saw your sister—if it's not too painful?"

"On Friday before the kidnapping, I met her for lunch at Sherry's on ...." She began sobbing again before she could finish the sentence.

Nolan put away his diary. "I'm very sorry, ma'am. Why don't we wait until another time."

"No, let's finish," She took a deep breath. "I had lunch with Sarah at Sherry's on Sixth Avenue. She and Colin .... Do you know who Colin is?"

"Colin Flannery."

"Yes, she planned to marry him. She wanted to tell me her plans, for that and for a business the two wanted to start. She was a very modern girl, and she wanted to get married in City Hall and then have a catered reception at her apartment. No expensive church wedding or anything like that. But Sarah was ... I don't like to say this, but she could be very foolish. Colin worked as a stevedore on the docks. No one in the family liked him. In fact, he's the person you should be examining the closest."

"He was at his job that day. I spoke to his boss and three people who worked with him. I also saw his time sheet."

"I don't care. Colin is a .... His reasons for courting Sarah were obvious. She had money. He didn't. The only person in the world who didn't seem to mind that was Sarah. Colin was a rough person and ... again, I don't like saying this when she's missing, but my theory is that Sarah wanted a man who would know his place. She had the money and position. He had neither. She counted on Colin being grateful for the rest of his life, being a loving husband and father. I don't think he would have been grateful at all. He just wanted her money."

Her eyes tearing again, she went to a table near the fireplace and took a fresh handkerchief from a drawer.

"You say she and Flannery wanted to start a business. What sort of business?"

"They planned to borrow money against her jewels to buy

fresh flowers brought in by the South American steamships in winter. They'd sell them in arrangements to the better florist shops around the city. Sarah liked flower arranging, and Colin said he knew about importing. He was going to quit his job on the docks to manage the business."

"On the day ... well, when this happened—"

"Saturday."

"Where were you?"

"In the morning, I drove up to my father's farm in White Plains. He was going to come up Sunday."

"You drove yourself? That's quite a trip. Those roads."

"I had a chauffeur. A man from—let me think—a man from South America, I believe. Not much English. He only worked for me that one time over the holidays, for the Christmas trip up to White Plains. The rest of the time, I stayed in the city and took taxis."

"Sorry I have to ask these things."

"It's what detectives do. I understand that. I could try to find him, if you think it's important."

Julia stood and began to cry again. "I stayed at the farm Saturday night. Then, Sunday afternoon, my father called with the terrible news, so we drove back to the city."

"I'm so sorry."

Sniffling into the handkerchief, she walked about the room.

Nolan turned pages in his diary. "Another question, if you don't mind. The jewels that were stolen ... did you know where they were in the apartment?"

"Sarah was so stupid about those jewels. Did my father tell you anything about them?"

"He made gifts to both of you, he said."

"Yes. Right away, I put mine in a bank deposit box, but Sarah, she and Colin planned to borrow against them for their business, so she kept these extremely valuable jewels—I mean thousands and thousands worth—she kept these jewels right there in the apartment."

"Did anyone know where she hid them?"

"Lots of people did. About a month before she was kidnapped, she gave a luncheon. I was there, my brother Timothy, my mother and stepfather—"

"Mr. Dutton."

"Yes, and during the dessert—"

"Was your father there? The captain?"

"Oh, God, no. My father in the same room as Colin, as my brother, as his ex-wife? God, God, no. My father despised Colin. Right in the middle of dessert, though, Colin was blathering on about the flower thing, the business, and Sarah blurted out where she kept the jewels. In a sock at the bottom of a steamer trunk in her closet. She thought it was preciously funny. All these diamonds and pearls and sapphires sitting in a woolen sock. Every one of us urged her to put them in the bank, even Colin. In fact, especially Colin. She just laughed about it. She liked them being in that sock. It was a hilarious joke to her. I can't imagine how many other people she told."

"You said your brother was there. I heard he had, uh, medical problems."

"No. He had a cocaine habit."

Nolan had to stifle a smile. "Should I talk to him?"

She glared at him. "You can talk to anyone you want, Mr. Nolan."

"I'm sorry, ma'am. I just meant, would he be able to cast any light on what happened?"

"Ask him yourself, but he was upstate at a treatment farm when it happened."

"I don't mean to upset you."

With a sigh, she sat down, reached over, and touched his arm. "You're not. I'm sorry. I know detectives have to be detectives."

"I won't talk to him, if you don't want me to."

She smiled at him. "You're a first. No policeman I've ever known would say, 'I won't do such and such if you don't want me to.'"

"I'm not a policeman."

"Sorry. Once a thing is in your mind, it's hard to get it out. In any case, you're quite the polite detective."

"Thank you."

"Finish your meal. You can still ask me your questions. Do you want some more of the sirloin?"

"No, thanks, this is fine." He took another bite with one hand while holding the diary in the other.

She rose to retrieve a fresh handkerchief from the table by the fireplace. Seemingly unaware that she stood beside the massive portrait of herself, she dabbed at her eyes and momentarily struck the same pose. With her face lit by the subdued glow from the fireplace, the scene and her beauty took Nolan's breath away.

She turned to see him staring at her. Nolan quickly focused on the diary again, but not before seeing her smile.

"Uh, one more thing about your brother, and I apologize for asking this ... did he need money at all?"

She returned to her chair and took a moment to think. "He did and he didn't. He was trying to be a painter and so he wanted to live like young painters do—you know, in impoverished conditions. He didn't need a lot of money to live like that. But he told me he just had a landscape accepted at the National Academy of Design and was going to be part of their winter exhibition here in the city. He thought his prospects were going to improve quickly. But if your mind is working toward the idea he hired this robber to get hold of her jewels, no. Absolutely not. My sister and brother were very close and protective of each other. It wouldn't have been in his nature to rob her and certainly not to hold her for ransom. Do you know about the new theories on human nature, Mr. Nolan? Is it John?"

"Yes, ma'am. John. And no, I didn't know there were any new theories."

"There's always new theories. You should attend some of the free lectures around the city."

"Maybe there's new theories, but there's no 'new human nature,' at least that I've found."

She smiled at this. He took the last bite of potatoes and wiped his mouth with the linen napkin. Carefully putting the plate and silverware on the side table, he refolded the napkin and laid it beside the plate.

"I'll tell you, Mr. Nolan. You've also got manners like no policeman I ever knew. They don't know what a napkin's for. They wipe their mouths on the back of their hands. Now let me ask you my own detective questions, if you don't mind. Where are you from in Ireland?"

"County Carlow, south of Dublin."

"And how long have you been in New York?

"About a year."

"And how about a girl, Mr. Nolan? I see you have a ring on your left hand. Does that mean you've got a wife?"

"No, it's just a ring. It honors one of my uncles. It was his."

"Well, if you're not married, there must be quite a few girls interested in your wellbeing. Do you have anyone who's special to you?"

Gates' office

10

A Fresh Lead

∾⌒

IN A DEEP sleep, Nolan first experienced the knocking as part of a dream. When it continued, its insistence roused him from his slumber. Finally Tierney's shouting and pounding on the door propelled him out of bed.

"Nolan, open up! Let's go!"

As Nolan opened the door to his flat, he saw that behind Tierney the door of the Spanish railroad brakeman across the landing had opened at the same time. Tierney turned to glare at the man. The sight of his holstered revolver and badge convinced the brakeman to shut it quickly.

"I'm not supposed to work today," Nolan said, rubbing his eyes. "I guarded Julia Dutton all night. I just got home a couple of hours ago. I need sleep."

"You're not going to get no sleep today. The captain just called. Someone tried to sell his girl's jewels at a pawnshop. Gates wants to see you."

"Why can't you go?"

"Gates says he wants *you*, and he's paying for your services, so it's going to be you, Nolan. I've got my motor outside, but I don't like your neighborhood, so I'll be downstairs waiting and guarding my Mitchell. And for God's sake, move somewhere where they got a phone in the hall."

"HERE HE IS, Captain. And just to mention it, because I had to go fetch him, there's going to be a charge for the—"

"For you, also. I know, Sean. Just send me the bill."

"A man has to keep up with the books, Captain. You know because you're in business."

Gates, who was holding a telephone receiver to his ear with one hand and a cigar with the other, dismissed him with a wave. Tierney tipped his bowler and politely backed out of the room. Gates motioned for Nolan to take a seat opposite his massive desk.

"It'll be a minute. I'm waiting on a call."

Nolan had never been in Gates' office, which was located on Times Square, on the fourth floor of a building with an elevator. More like a room in a Renaissance palace than an office, it featured an intricately carved stone mantelpiece at one end, walls of variously colored marble, gilded molding, and a huge framed map of Manhattan opposite Gates' desk. Through the window behind Gates, Nolan could see across the square to where a steel girder was being raised by ropes and winches to the roof of an unfinished building.

"You know," Gates said, "I own this building. I bought the property twenty years ago for fifty-seven thousand. It was a trolley barn in those days, but I tore it down and built this. What do you think it's worth today?"

A voice apparently came on the line and Gates listened a moment. " 'Dear,' he called me," he said into the mouthpiece. "So why should I hold the wire? You go get him right now. You tell him if he doesn't come on the line in fifteen seconds, I'm hanging up." Gates put the earpiece to his chest and took a puff on his cigar. "There was a news item last week. A banker, he gets a call from a man says he's invented a device to attach to a telephone so you can take an instant photograph of who you're talking to right through the wires. The banker says, 'Prove it.' The caller says, 'I see you're smoking a cigar.' By God, this banker almost writes him an investment check till he figures it out. Every banker smokes cigars. The man was just guessing."

Gates glanced at the clock and then slammed the earpiece back into its holder.

"Stupid," Gates muttered. "Did Tierney tell you anything?"

"The pawnshop."

"Yes, on Lexington. What's too bad is the dumb store owner told the man that police were looking for a brooch just like the one he was offering, so the man ran out. But I have a description of him."

He pushed a paper across the desk, which Nolan read.

"It's the same as what the two women on the alley saw," Nolan said.

"Here's what I think," Gates said, crushing out the stub of his cigar. "No, first you tell me what you think."

Nolan considered this new information for a moment.

"My guess is the police put out a description of the jewels to all the pawnshops in Manhattan. But now the kidnapper knows this. He won't bring it to another in Manhattan. He'll go up to Westchester or over to New Jersey—"

"Or up to Connecticut or out to Long Island," Gates said. "Exactly what I thought. Very good. Here, look at this." He passed another sheet to Nolan. "I had fifty of these printed up. A description of the jewels, the man, everything. You get a list of the pawnshops—"

"Sir, he got rid of Sarah's Packard. So he probably doesn't have a motor. People who need money, which it sounds like he does, don't keep motors. My guess is he'll take surface lines to get to pawnshops and only those as far as a day trip. I don't think going up to Connecticut is likely or going past Queens on Long Island."

Gates leaned back in his chair. "You're right. Very good again. Start with the shops outside Manhattan but near the surface lines. Can you do that?"

Nolan stood and took the handbills.

"After you get through these pawnshops, talk to a police detective, name of Cochran, at the 42nd Street Station. You know him?"

"I know his name. He was on duty the Sunday they found your daughter was missing. He wrote the report."

"He knows you're contacting him. He'll give you the latest evidence. And here. This is ten dollars extra. For your expenses. I already paid off Cochran, so don't give him nothing and don't tell Tierney or he'll want his cut."

"Captain, I appreciate this a great deal. Thank you."

"And thank you. If my poor Sarah is found, I'll bet you're the one that finds her. I pray to God you can." The meeting apparently over, Gates started to reach for his telephone to make another call, but he suddenly laughed. "One more thing.

No, two more things. One is Julia called me this morning."

He did not immediately finish the thought, eyeing Nolan for his reaction.

"Yes, sir?"

"You upset her," he said, but he was smiling broadly.

"How did I—"

"You told her you have an intended you love deeply and you hope to bring her over from Ireland so you can marry her."

"Yes, sir."

Gates again said nothing, but his smile turned to silent laughter that made his chest heave.

"You told my very rich daughter, my very beautiful daughter—whose apartment you were sitting in, whose food you were eating, who you had talked to for quite a length of time she tells me, and who clearly thought something of you, Nolan—you told her that you love this other girl in Ireland, this poor girl in Ireland, more than anything in the world."

"I suppose I did."

"You don't see how that can upset a woman?"

"I suppose I do, but it couldn't be helped, sir. It was the truth."

Gates shook his head and picked up the telephone earpiece, preparing to make a call. "John, you're a damn interesting fellow."

Nolan began to leave but turned.

"What's the other thing, captain? You said two things."

"Oh. This building." Gates slapped his free hand down hard on the desk. "Worth one and a half million today. Go figure that as a percentage profit, if you want to amuse yourself."

Crosse & Smith Pawnshop

11

The Pawnshop

꣑

NOLAN SPENT SEVERAL days distributing the handbills about the stolen jewels to pawnshops on the periphery of New York's network of trolleys, ferries, and railroad lines, from New Jersey to Long Island. Eleven shops in all.

On Monday afternoon, returning to the agency office, he found a note from Tierney saying a promising call had come in from a pawnshop in Newark. The brooch had been brought in there.

Tuesday morning at eight o'clock, Nolan was waiting outside Crosse & Smith's pawnshop on Market Street in Newark. He took one of the Hudson River ferries to reach it.

Soon the owner arrived. "You the detective?"

"Yes, sir. You called about a stolen brooch?"

The owner, whose eyeglasses were so thick Nolan could barely tell if the man had eyes, unlocked the multiple bolt locks and pushed the door open—but not before looking up and down the sidewalk for anything suspicious. Once inside, he locked the door behind them and placed a sign in the window: "Admittance by permission only. Knock first."

"Excuse my caution, but we've been robbed twice in a week," he said. "The first time, they got in after midnight but couldn't drill into the safe, so two nights later, they came back with dynamite."

Inside, Nolan could see no evidence of an explosion. There

were shelves, cases, and display tables full of clocks, coins, and jewelry.

"What'd they blow up?"

There was a knock at the store's front door. The owner peered through the glass and admitted an elderly woman with a valise, locking it again behind her.

"What you got today, dear?"

"Let me show you."

"Just a minute. First, I got this young man."

The owner took Nolan out to the office in back, where he searched for the handbill in a stack of other papers on his desk.

"You wanna know what they blew up? Nothing. See that coil of wire in the corner? It's a slow fuse. They brought a hundred feet of it but forgot to bring a simple penknife to cut it. They had the dynamite all set to go on the safe but no short fuse. So they decided to light the whole coil and wait outside in the alley for it to blow. Lucky someone saw them and called the police. When the wagon got here, the fuse wasn't even a third of the way there. It would've been next Sunday before the job was done."

Finally, he located the handbill.

"All right. So this fellow comes in yesterday and shows me a brooch. I make him an offer, but he says he'll have to think about it and will come back today. I checked your handbill and realized it had the etched initials on the back like it says here, SWD. Someone had tried to scratch them out with a file, but the etching was deep. You could still read them. I knew this was who you're looking for, but your sheet here, it doesn't say anything about the reward."

"I'm sure there will be one."

"You're sure? *Sure?* That means there won't be."

"I can't speak for the owner."

"Why not? You're his detective."

Nolan thought. "All right. There'll be a reward."

"How much?"

"I don't know."

"That still means there won't be."

"Twenty dollars then."

Incredulous, the owner shook his head. "I know the value of things. That brooch was five thousand if it wasn't six or eight."

"Fifty dollars then."

The owner again shook his head.

"Honestly," Nolan said. "I can't speak for the owner."

"Then the information you need to catch this man, which I have more of than what I told you, is going to cost you a hundred dollars."

Nolan thought again. "Do you have a telephone?"

"Right here."

The owner went back into the shop as Nolan lifted the earpiece to call Gates. Fifteen minutes later, having lost an open line to Manhattan twice, Nolan waited for another. He heard a knock on the store's front door, and from where he stood, he could see the customer through the door's glass window. About forty, blond hair, maybe five feet six. Nolan knew this was the man.

He replaced the phone, and with as leisurely a walk as he could force himself to make, he went back into the shop's main room. Behind his back, he transferred his ring to his left hand.

The owner, who could not see the customer's face from the approach he took to the door, finally did and immediately glanced back at Nolan with the confirmation Nolan wanted in his eyes.

The owner slipped the bolt and let him in.

"I'm hoping you'll take another look at the piece I showed you yesterday and decide maybe your offer should be raised up."

"Why would I do that? You went some other places and found out my offer was the best you got."

"I don't think it's fair, though. Just take another look."

Nolan, his heart pounding, pretended to be browsing the display cases. The woman with the valise had taken a chair and appeared to be napping as she waited.

"I looked at it already," the owner said as he moved behind the counter. From where Nolan stood, he could see the owner's hand close around a small pistol that was sitting on a shelf beneath the cash register.

"I'm just asking that you examine it again," the suspect said, taking a handkerchief from his pocket that apparently wrapped the brooch. "It's a fine piece. Did you count the diamonds?"

"I counted them ... but what you didn't count on is I know it's stolen." The owner slapped Nolan's handbill in front of the man, pointing to the description of the brooch. Then he brought the pistol up above the counter and leveled it at him.

As if he had only been asked politely to leave, the blond man slowly returned the handkerchief to his pocket, crumpled the handbill, and put that in his pocket. Then he walked toward the door with no special haste.

Nolan, who had been transfixed by it all, realized he had to act.

"Hey! I'm a detective! Don't move!"

The man broke toward the door, which had not been relocked, and even though Nolan feared the owner was about to shoot, he made a grab for the blond man and got hold of one wrist. The man yanked his arm away and kicked at Nolan, catching him in the kneecap. Then he was out the door and down the sidewalk.

Nolan, numbed to the pain and spurred on by the excitement, ran after him. He quickly closed the gap between them, despite patches of snow on the sidewalk. Within a dozen strides, he was on top of him. Nolan took him down by hooking an arm around his throat and kicking his legs out from beneath him.

Once on the pavement, they tussled, with the man viciously kicking at Nolan and trying to gouge Nolan's eye with his thumb. Furious, Nolan brought his ring down on his temple with all the force he could manage, causing him to scream in pain and stop struggling. Blood streamed down his face. Using a choke lock on his neck, Nolan held him in place.

Hearing the commotion, people came out of the line of shops and a crowd rapidly formed. Four men, apparently thinking they were referees at a prize fight, tried to pry the combatants apart.

Nolan swung at them as well. "I'm a detective! Don't let him up! Private detective! Private detective!"

With one hand momentarily free, he tried to pull his badge from his coat pocket, but it fell onto the pavement and skittered to the curb. Undeterred, the men grabbed at both of them, trying to free Nolan's arm lock.

"What's he done? Skipped alimony?"

"Didn't he pay his taxes?"

"Damn detectives!"

Now they were mainly grabbing at Nolan, and the blond man was coming loose from his grasp.

"He thinks I'm someone I'm not!" the blond man yelled. "I didn't do nothing!"

Apparently convinced Nolan was the villain in this, one of the men began kicking him. Another joined in. In a moment, the blond man was free and running down the sidewalk as Nolan tried to protect himself from the men's brutal kicks.

TIERNEY WAS WAITING for him outside New York Hospital on West 15th, but not in his personal motor, the Mitchell. He was in the agency's official machine, a beat-up black Ford. Nolan had made it back to Manhattan before he realized his injuries might be worse than he thought.

"Anything broke, Cousin?"

"They don't know. They wrapped my ribs anyway." Nolan gingerly eased himself into the passenger seat.

"You should've had a revolver. Didn't I tell you?"

"He didn't have a gun and I got him down with no trouble. But a mob took over."

"At least you know what he looks like now. I told Gates you only saw the man and chased him, but he got away. That's all I told him."

"If there was no mob ...."

Tierney looked over at Nolan, who was feeling his ribs. "This place we're going to is uptown. You gonna be able to do this when we get there?"

Nolan raised and lowered his arms several times. "Feels good enough."

Tierney pulled the Ford out into heavy traffic, mostly other Fords and motor trucks.

"If you had a revolver and drew it, you think this mob would have been on you?"

"What am I going to do? Shoot everyone in the mob?"

"Well, you would've had six bullets. Was there more than six of them?"

Nolan saw Tierney look over, waiting for him to laugh. He did not. With the laudanum wearing off, the aching in his ribs had returned. He closed his eyes. Could things be any worse? If he had held on to the man, Sarah might be free right now.

They took Fifth Avenue north, passing sidewalks full of women entering or exiting department stores and other shops.

They reached the city yards at 56th Street, a paved lot where the police stored wagons and motor-delivery trucks confiscated for legal reasons. It was largely empty, save for the small brick building in the far corner that housed the pound officer. The day had warmed, leaving puddles of water where patches of Ice and snow had been in the morning.

The driving instructor waited for them outside the gate.

"I'm Mr. Biddinger," the instructor said, extending his hand to Nolan. "You the fella—"

"That's gonna learn to drive, yes," said Tierney.

"Ever driven a motor before?"

"No, sir," Nolan said.

Taking the wheel, Biddinger motioned Nolan to climb into the passenger seat. Tierney got in the back.

"That's good," he said as he slowly drove into the lot. "I'll have a chance to instill proper habits in you. If the police drive something into the yards—and they usually don't this late on a Saturday—my man inside is going to signal us to stop right where we are, especially if it's a horse and wagon, as some horses still don't like motors. The first thing I want to show you is the brake. This pedal here. You see it?"

"I see it."

"So, you're one of Mr. Tierney's detectives?"

"I am, yes."

"Notice how I changed gears into first right there? You shift this hand lever into the second position, which is this one—"

"I see it."

"And you push the clutch pedal all the way down, which is your gear selector. What kind of cases you boys work on?'

"Cases where this man needs to know how to drive," Tierney said. "You pay someone inside the yards for the privilege of using it?"

"No, my brother leases this land to the city, so they let me use it sometimes. Notice I have the hand throttle set at a slow speed."

"He's got to learn high-speed driving eventually. Where do you take him to learn that?"

"I've got some streets up in the Bronx."

"What speeds are we talking about?" Nolan asked.

"I've seen police chases get up near forty miles per hour," Biddinger said. "Right on city streets."

Nolan groaned, causing Tierney to laugh.

"And you've got be able to drive and shoot your revolver out a window at the same time, if it comes to that," Tierney said.

"You don't pay me enough."

Nolan glanced back to see Tierney glaring at him. When the engine stalled, Biddinger got out to check the water. Tierney leaned over the front seat, menacingly close to Nolan's ear.

"I'm warning you," he whispered. "Don't imply I'm cheap to anyone. I pay you the going rate for new Irish. You understand?"

"I was joking."

"Well, I'm not."

The detective examines the sledgehammer

12

The Police Detective

❦

DETECTIVE COCHRAN HAD a desk in a rear office of the 42nd Street Station House. He shared the room with a half dozen other detectives. Nolan recognized Cochran from an evidence photo in which he displayed the sledgehammer that was used by the robber to gain entrance.

Nolan stood by his desk, but Cochran did not look over.

"Sir?"

Busy writing, Cochran kept his eyes on his work. "What?"

"Captain Gates told me to see you."

"My captain is Rosenberg."

"Captain Gates. The Dutton case."

He glanced up. "Oh, yeah. What's he captain of anyway? A hotel staff somewhere? Take a seat. I'll be with you."

Nolan guessed he was in his fifties, though he had the type of round, featureless face that had probably looked that age at twenty-five. A walrus mustache covered his mouth. He was filling out police forms, and judging by his sighs and shrugs as he scratched in the information with a fountain pen, each entry was a terrible labor. A new Remington typewriter sat under a stack of other forms at the corner of his desk. Nolan guessed that the younger policemen used the machines; the older ones resisted.

He finally laid the forms aside. "The family hired you, huh."

"Yes."

"What for?" His voice had a cold edge. Cochran stared at Nolan, who did not immediately have an answer.

"What do you think police do all day while you're running around with your fake badges?" Cochran said. "We try to solve crimes, but we got dozens of 'em, not just one or two like you people."

Nolan had no response to that either.

"This is how it's going to be," the detective said. "Sure, you go ahead and investigate anything you want, but if you find anything, you bring it to me first, not Gates. I don't want you messing up any line of investigation I have going. You understand?"

Nolan nodded.

"It clear?"

"I guess so."

Cochran stuck his finger in Nolan's chest.

"You don't *guess* nothing. You know so."

"Then I guess I know so."

Cochran sneered. He reached across his desk and found a file in a stack.

"Gates said he's been able to stall making the ransom payment to this man. That right?"

Nolan nodded.

"He also told me you tracked down a pawnshop in New Jersey where one of the jewels was brought in. That so?"

"Yes."

"Did the shoppie get a get a good look at him?"

"Did he ... did the shop owner see him?"

"What do you think I'm asking? Yeah. Did the shoppie see his face?"

"I ... uh ... yes. The details he gave me matched the description of the man given by the two women looking out on the alley."

Cochran opened the file folder and took out several sheets of paper.

"I got here a copy of the list of the pawnshops we contacted. You can have it and copies of the notes from a few more interviews we done of people in the Dutton girl's building and such. You give me your list of pawnshops you visit, and if you interview anyone we missed, you write it all down and give me a copy. You understand?"

Nolan nodded. Cochran pushed the papers across the desk

to Nolan but kept his hand on them. "You got something for me first?"

Nolan did not understand.

"I'm not giving you this for nothing."

"I thought Captain Gates paid you."

Cochran grimaced. "Don't say 'paid,' you fool, and don't say nothing but in a whisper. And when you figure out what I mean and you go into your wallet, do it inside your coat so no one sees it. And whatever you takes out, put it under that book at your elbow so no one sees that either. You understand?"

Nolan leveled a glare at Cochran until he thought better of it and let it fade. *Do not anger the police*, he told himself. Reluctantly, he stood to take his wallet out of his back pocket. As if challenged, Cochran stood too, making it clear that he was considerably taller and bulkier, and judging by the look on his face, meaner.

WHEN NOLAN RETURNED to the agency, Tierney and three of his detectives were just coming down the front steps.

"Nolan, we need you. You ride with me."

He drove uptown with Tierney in his roadster. The other three went in the Ford. A photograph was in Tierney's lap.

"You ever been on a shadow detail?"

"No," Nolan said.

"We got a man we're tailing that will know he's being tailed if one man does it alone. So four of you is gonna do it. You're gonna get in a line behind him and once in a while trade places. That way, if the man turns, he won't see the same man all the time. You got it?"

"I guess."

"Do you got it or not?"

"I got it, Sean. What's this man done? Is that him in the photo?"

Tierney handed him the photograph. The face in the photo was of a balding man in his forties, wearing eyeglasses. "His name's Sipping. We don't know he's done nothin'. His wife thinks he has, though. She's paying us to see where he goes coming out of work each day. He told her he works to six. She found out he only works to five. Personally, I think he sits in a bar for an hour to avoid having to go home."

At Times Square, they turned north onto Broadway.

Eventually, Tierney pulled the Mitchell to the curb opposite a haberdasher's shop at Broadway and 66th. His three detectives were already across the street, two in the Ford and one on the sidewalk, ready to begin the procession.

They sat in silence. Tierney took out a pocket watch and glanced at it. After showing it to Nolan, he returned it to his vest pocket. Eight minutes to five.

"When Sipping comes out, you gotta get your arse across the street and fall in the back of the line. So don't get comfortable," Tierney said. "By the way, a friend of yours called. He saw you at the tube station in New Jersey a couple of days ago getting on a train. Said he knew you from before, the old days. He said he's been trying to track you down. Couldn't remember your name, but described you."

"He asked for me?"

"Yeah, some friend from before. I took it to mean from Ireland. I said that's where you came from. He said, yeah, he met you on the steamer making the passage."

"But I didn't make any friends on the passage. We were all too busy being sick."

"Well, he said he knows you."

"He saw me at the tube station? On the train?"

"That's what he said."

"I've been to New Jersey only once in the last month, to that pawnshop, and I took the ferry both ways."

"Don't know anything about it. He called and said what he said."

"If he couldn't find me, how'd he get your number?" Suddenly Nolan remembered the handbill. At the pawnshop, the man with the brooch took it from the shopkeeper, balled it up, and stuffed it in his pocket before heading out the door. It had the agency's telephone number on it.

"Sean, what'd you tell him?" There was urgency in his voice.

"You watching the door for Sipping?"

"Sean, what did you tell this man who called? Did you tell him my name?"

"I reminded him of it, yeah. He says, sure, John Nolan. That's him. He wanted your telephone number to get back in touch. I told him you don't have none, so's I gave him your address."

"You gave him my *address*? Where I *live*?"

"He said he was a friend. When he comes by, you'll recognize him, I'm sure. Are you watching the door, dammit?"

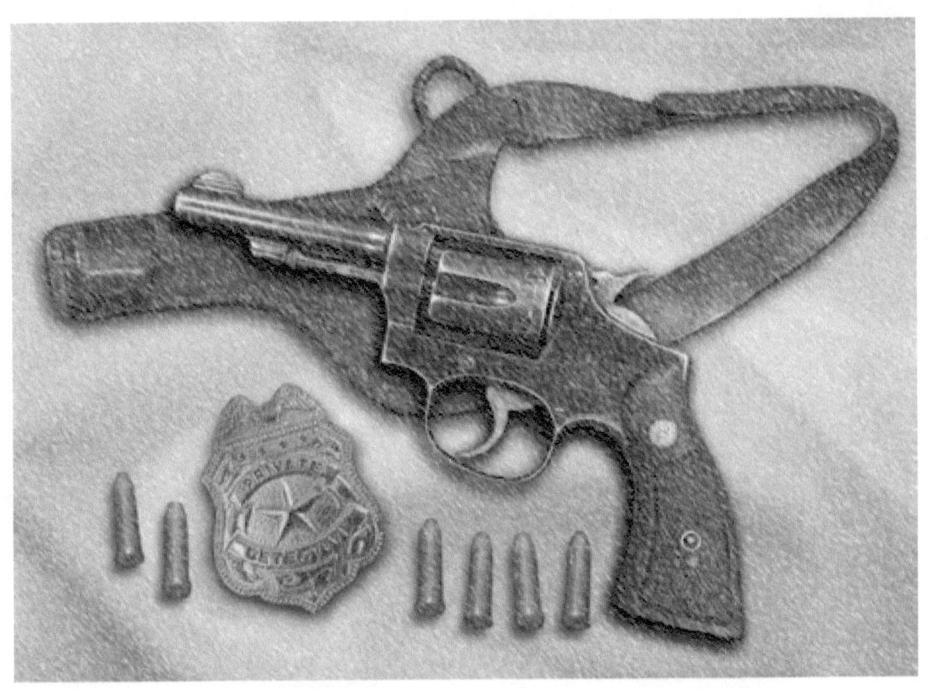

The Smith & Wesson military and police revolver

13

Fears in the Night

❧

THE FRENCHMAN HAD begun working a second shift at a furniture factory in the Bronx. He would usually come home between eleven and midnight.

Lying in bed in the dark and waiting for his roommate's return, Nolan listened to the echoing of the footsteps on the bare wooden stairs in the stairwell. A kitchen knife was hidden under his pillow. However, the steps ended on a lower floor.

Nolan thought about removing his name from the mailboxes in the first-floor hall. Should he go that far? Would fear rule his life now?

He tried to recall how hard he had hit the blond man with his ring. It drew blood, but was it a sideways hit that had not cut too deeply? Or was it a deep wound that left a permanent scar? Thinking about it now, he was sure it was a powerful hit that had left a mark. This was going to be revenge for a scar, he was certain.

The lock on their apartment door barely worked. The bolt did not go all the way into the metal slot, and with no effort at all, the door could be forced open. At one point, he got up and wedged a kitchen chair beneath the door handle. Back in bed, he realized that if he fell asleep before the Frenchman returned, the man would raise a commotion throughout the building, trying to get in. He took the chair away but still fell asleep before the Frenchman got back.

What worried him most the next morning was that he never heard him come in.

"YOU EVER FIRED a revolver in your life?"

"I've handled them and seen them fired," Nolan said. "My father had one."

"But you never fired one."

"No."

Tierney took a brand-new Smith & Wesson military and police six-shooter from its box on his desk. A left-handed shoulder holster made of leather and a box of thirty-two caliber bullets were alongside.

"Why'd you change your mind about carrying this?"

"A lot of reasons."

"That mob in New Jersey put the fear of God in you, I bet."

"That's one reason."

"Okay, there's no bullets in it yet, so you can't kill anyone right at the moment, Cousin. But here's six bullets. They're for practice."

Nolan took the handful of bullets.

"Now listen closely," Tierney said. "There's a shooting range in Cypress Hills in Brooklyn. They know me, so they'll give you the detective's rate if you show them your badge. I want you to go over there this evening to make sure you shoot this revolver before you ever have to pull it for real. I'm gonna load one bullet for you to show you how it's done. See? The cylinder rolls out like this. Then like this, the bullet goes in the chamber."

"Move your hand."

"Like this. Slips right in. Then you snap the cylinder closed. When you're at the range, get a receipt. Tomorrow morning, I want you to come back with all six empty casings and show me, 'cuz we gotta go to my insurance man and show him the casings and your receipt. You gotta sign a paper, then we gotta go before a magistrate and get you a license to carry. You know why I'm so tough about this?"

"Why?"

"Two years ago, I'd hired a man named Dozier, who was chasing a man around Columbus Circle. Dozier never bothered to take shooting practice and sign the paper like I told him. He just went right out with the revolver. So he's chasing this man around the circle in the middle of the day and starts firing and hits someone else, not the man he's aiming at. He hit this other poor man in the foot. I would have been on the hook personally, because of no signed insurance paper, but the man with the foot must have been avoiding the police about something. He limped off before the ambulance ever got there. Lucky, incredibly lucky."

Tierney handed him the revolver, the six bullets, and the shoulder holster.

"Here, take it. When you bring back the casings, I'll give you six more bullets That's all the free ones you're gonna get. You buy your own bullets after that."

"I'll go to the range this afternoon." Nolan held up the revolver. "You got something I can carry this in?"

"Yeah, in the holster, like God intended. Strap it on. Carry the bullets in your pocket."

Smiling like a proud father, Tierney watched him attach the straps of the shoulder holster and then slip the Smith & Wesson into it and close his suit jacket. Barely a bulge.

"There you go, Nolan. You're officially a detective."

Pennsylvania Station

14

The Payment

❧

January 6, 1915

Dear Mr. Gates,

Sarah has been moved to a cabin in the mountains where she is being treated well and fed well by my friends. Each day she gets to go outside and walk around and get fresh air. So we are keeping up our end. And now it's time for you to keep up your end.

On this Friday at noon, go to the main waiting room of Pennsylvania Station and put the money in a paper bag and drop it in the big garbage can by the north staircase. I'll be watching. Don't tell police. If I see anyone nearby that looks suspicious like a policeman I won't pick it up. Then Sarah will lose her life. NO POLICE!!!

If I pick it up and I'm nabbed by a policeman then my friends will kill Sarah at sunset if I am not back.

Do what I say exactly or this will be the end for Sarah.

After I get the money, I will call you at five in the afternoon about where to find your daughter.

This is her signature below. Will it be the last time she ever writes her name? This is up to you.

Sarah

By late Friday morning, Pennsylvania Station was only mildly busy. The massive Beaux-Arts building served trains connecting to other cities across the country. In the main waiting room, police detectives, all male, were dressed in a variety of disguises, both as males and females. A cleaning woman with a pail and mop. A Pennsylvania Railroad clerk at the information desk. An elderly woman with her luggage on a bench. A uniformed conductor, calling out the trains and track numbers.

At noon, Captain Gates entered the station from Seventh Avenue, through the pink-granite colonnade, carrying a paper bag filled with a few hundred-dollar bills but mostly blank paper slips tied in bundles.

The plan was to grab the man who retrieved the sack and then to sweat him hard for Sarah's location. ("If we pay him and let him leave, that's as good as a death sentence for my daughter.")

The police agreed. However, no one—except for a child who threw away a paper napkin—went near the garbage can in the hour after the money was put into it. The detective dressed as the cleaning woman finally emptied the can and retrieved the sack at one o'clock.

At five o'clock, the telephone call came to Gates' office. The police had connected a switch to the line that allowed two other officers to listen. Gates demanded that one of those listeners be Nolan.

"I was there," Gates said. "I put the money in the can, just like you instructed."

"I never planned to pick it up. I just wanted to see if you'd be there and you were. I saw you go in with the bag. And I didn't see no policemen. But like I said, this was just a test. Now this is what I want you to do. You take the—"

"The money is gone! They've emptied that can by now. I never went back, and there were no police there. I did exactly what you said."

The caller, who had continued to maintain an unnaturally high-pitched voice, fell silent for a moment. "I figured you'd go back and check in an hour and pick up your money when it was still there."

"I did what you said! I left and waited for this call. Where's my daughter? That was the agreement. Where is she?"

The caller was silent.

"I want to know if she's alive!" Gates demanded.

"She's alive."

"How do I know that?"

"Because, well, because I'm a businessman, like you. It doesn't make no sense for me to kill her. I'd get nothing. And it doesn't make no sense for you not to pay. Or else you know I'd kill her. So we're working together in this."

"If you want another fifty-thousand dollars, I have to do the same thing again. I have to get another bank loan on my properties, and that's going to take time."

"Your daughter will be treated good, I promise. In fact, I've grown to like her. But I'm a patient man, so I'm willing to wait for however long it takes for us to finish this transaction to both our satisfactions. I'll call you next week. You just get the money."

Robert T. Dutton

15

The Stepfather

 ⚮

"**J**OHN NOLAN! MESSAGE for John Nolan!"

"I'm John Nolan."

The bellboy handed him a small envelope. The Biltmore lobby was busy, so Nolan moved away from the flow of people to a quiet corner and a wing chair, where he took out the note.

> Mrs. Dutton is indisposed. However, I'll be in the dining room for a late lunch in 15 minutes, should you want to join me for a talk.

The included card was signed, *Robert Train Dutton.*

One of the most sumptuous hotels in the city and the world, the Biltmore was a stone and brick edifice of twenty-six stories. Adjacent to Grand Central Terminal, it had its own arrival station for the rich. The hotel was often in the news due to the prominence of the people who stayed there—presidents, kings, industrialists, entertainers.

Approaching the main dining room, Nolan received a suspicious glance from the maître d'. He showed the man the card and—after a grudging smile of apology with just a hint of disapproval—he was taken to a small table by the window. Two red-tasseled menus, one for lunch, the other for dinner, were placed at its center.

Looking around and seeing no one else in a hat, Nolan

quickly removed his. How many other social gaffes would he make in this hotel before lunch was over?

The palatial room was certainly intimidating. Pilasters of pink-veined marble ran up the walls to the two-story-high ceiling. The furniture was dark oak. The carpet, upholstery, and window draperies were dark red.

The menu was just as intimidating: *Caviar d'Astrakhan; blinis à la Russe; grenadins of veal, Neapolitan; croquettes, Livonienne.* There were no prices given. That meant he couldn't afford them. Aside from his inability to pay for any of it, how could he order what he could not pronounce?

"Mr. Nolan?"

Nolan turned and then rose quickly from his seat. "Mr. Dutton?"

"Please, go ahead and sit. Let's have some lunch."

Dutton was upright and elegant with a gleaming waxed handlebar mustache. Taking a chair, he snapped his linen napkin open, threw it in his lap, and eagerly opened his menu as if he had not eaten in days.

"I hope you're hungry. Wonderful chef here."

"Sir, I don't think I'm going to eat, if you don't mind."

Dutton lowered the menu to look at him. "Oh, I know what you're thinking. How does someone who's not a millionaire afford this food? You're absolutely right, so lunch is on me."

Nolan began to protest, but was stopped with a wave.

"You want to talk to me, then you have to lunch with me," Dutton said. "That's my rule."

Nolan smiled. "Thank you very much."

"And forgive my wife. She's very upset, as any mother would be with all that's happened. You can understand."

They studied their menus and Nolan did some quick arithmetic. Dutton appeared to be in his late thirties. Gates had to be close to sixty. The ex-Mrs. Gates, with a daughter nearly twenty-one, had to be at least forty, more likely over fifty.

He tried to form no judgment of any of this. It was a reality of the rich. Poor couples were usually close in age. Often, the rich were not. Rich men married younger women, and rich women married younger men. He tried to guard against generalities in his thinking, but there were some that could not be denied.

Nolan was able to look past his menu at Dutton without seeming conspicuous about it. He had taken two companies into bankruptcy, but it did not show on his face. The insulation of his wife's money apparently kept bad news from affecting him.

"Just so you know," Dutton said, "I'm only talking to you because my wife's daughter recommended it. She says you're a gentleman and took it upon yourself to sit outside her door to safeguard her life. Well, that deserves lunch, in my opinion."

The waiter arrived. Nolan's palms sweated as he looked over the menu.

"The duck and the *Salade Japonaise*," Dutton said. "And a glass of good white wine. You choose."

Both the waiter and Dutton looked at Nolan. Dutton seemed to see his difficulty.

"Give Mr. Nolan the duck and salad, but make his tea. I assume he's still working for the rest of the day."

"Very good, sir." The waiter graciously backed away from the table.

"I understand you're a private detective and have been hired to find the person who committed this crime," Dutton said.

"Yes, sir." Nolan took out his leather diary. "These questions are going to be blunt, sir, so I apologize for any awkwardness they create."

"Julia said you're quite the polite young man. Good for you."

"Sir, I understand you were in South America when the kidnapping took place."

"Off the coast. I can't even tell you exactly where—only the skipper can do that. We were aboard a private yacht."

Nolan wrote in the diary while Dutton watched him.

"Personally, I don't like being on the ocean," Dutton said. "However, my wife does, and I try to please her."

His wine came, and with two large gulps, the glass was quickly on its way to being drained.

"Sir, when was the last time you saw Sarah?"

"I believe it was a lunch at her apartment that she gave a few weeks before she, uh … before the crime. I'm guessing you know she planned to marry."

"Yes. Colin Flannery."

"He was there. Mrs. Dutton and I were too. Sarah's sister and her brother, Timothy, were also present."

Now a pair of waiters set salads in front of them. Dutton, holding his not-yet-empty glass of wine, snapped his fingers at one of the departing waiters. "And another glass of whatever this was, please."

Something caught Dutton's eye past Nolan. "Look behind you," he said.

Nolan turned.

"You know who that is? The table with the three men? The man with his back to you? Rube Marquard, the pitcher for the Giants." Dutton attacked his salad with gusto. "Last year, Henry Ford had a suite right on our floor one weekend. I rode the elevator with him."

Nolan moved on, turning a page in the diary. "Sir, I understand that during the lunch, Sarah mentioned where she kept her jewels. Is that right?"

"The jewels? Let me think. Did she mention where she kept her jewels?" He took another bite of the greens as he pondered the question. "I know there were a couple of arguments during the lunch, and I think one of them may have been about her hiding place. Yes, I think she did mention it."

"Do you recall where that was? It's just for my notes."

"Do I recall? Let me think." He took a moment. "She might have said they were in a sock somewhere."

"A sock in a drawer?"

"It could have been a drawer."

"Could it have been ... somewhere else? A sock in a closet maybe?"

"Could have been in a closet. I don't recall."

Nolan wrote in his diary. "You mentioned there was another argument .... Do you remember what it was about?"

"Well, let's see." He chewed a bit as he recalled. "It involved Timothy. Sarah refused—"

"The argument was between Sarah and Timothy?"

"Yes. Timothy, you might know, is an artist. Not very good, in my opinion, but don't tell my wife I said that." The duck was set down in front of them, a waiter on each plate. A third set down a pot of tea. "Timothy needed money for supplies and rent. But Gates didn't give him any jewels, as he did with the daughters. He didn't approve of his son's direction in life, to be honest. So Timothy wanted Sarah to be his patron."

"To sponsor him, to pay his way."

"Yes. He didn't see any reason she shouldn't sell a diamond or two. He said it would have paid his costs for a year, the way he lived in the Tenderloin, and he didn't feel it would be anything to Sarah."

"But she said no."

"She had a business venture in mind, and she said she needed all the jewels for that, so that's the reason she gave for refusing. But Colin mentioned, uh, something else—a problem Timothy had."

"Cocaine?"

"So you know about that. Yes, Colin mentioned the cocaine and, well, the argument blew up from that."

"Then it was Timothy and Colin who argued?"

"Sarah, Colin, Mrs. Dutton, Julia .... Oh God, it was *everybody* arguing with Timothy. He got so hostile that he stood up and left. But ten minutes later he came back and pleaded some more. It was decided, while he was gone, that if he got no money, it might force him to end his habit. It was also decided that if he went upstate for treatment, he might be advanced some money. When he came back in, we gave him the choice."

"What did he say to that?"

"He was *still* furious. He didn't like either choice. He made some speech about who do you people think you are trying to control my life. Then he stomped out again, the snip. Believe it or not, he came back a *third* time, distraught and begging for money. Finally, he agreed to the farm upstate."

Nolan recorded more notes. Dutton leaned forward slightly, trying to read what he was writing, until Nolan looked up. Dutton went back to his plate.

"Can you tell me anything about Sarah that might help me understand her?" Nolan asked.

"Such as what?"

"Such as what kind of girl she is. If she is being held somewhere, is this something she has the character to endure?"

"You mean is she a weak girl."

" 'Weak' may not be the right word."

"Sarah is a ... complicated girl, to be honest. Very headstrong. I'm sure she's quite strong enough to endure this hardship—if she's not killed by these men."

"You think it's men? Not one man?"

"Of course, I don't know," Dutton said. "I just assumed. But maybe it is one man."

Nolan wrote in his diary, something Dutton did not miss.

"Can I ask, why do you think she was interested in Colin? As I understand it, he's quite poor and a longshoreman. Seems an odd match."

"Julia has a theory. She thinks Sarah wanted a man who would be grateful for what she gave him and be a good husband. Sarah had money, so she didn't need his. These jewels her father gave her ... has anyone told you what they're worth?"

"No."

"My guess is close to eighty thousand dollars, maybe more. This business she and Colin were planning—she was very optimistic about it, naively optimistic from my perspective in the business world. She was convinced she was never going to need money again."

Dutton cleared his throat and paused, as if considering his next words carefully.

"I just want to say a few things that you may or may not have heard," he said. "It's about the captain, uh, Mr. Gates. He continues to be very bitter about the divorce. His point of view is that she, my wife, got much too much in the settlement. Don't tell my wife I told you this, but Gates left her for a young woman who urged Gates to get a divorce. He made the settlement with Mrs. Dutton so it would be fast. No one forced it on him. Ironically, the young woman found someone else in the meantime and left Gates, so that's an interesting story by itself. Gates lost quite a lot and got very little in return. Not that he doesn't have all the money he needs. He makes another fortune every year that goes by."

Dutton looked at Nolan as if expecting him to respond, but there was nothing Nolan could think of to say.

"The reason I'm telling you this, you see, is that Gates is living in a, well, in a cauldron of brewing emotions, in my opinion. He's mad at Mrs. Dutton because of the divorce. He's mad at his son because he's a painter. He was mad at Sarah because of Flannery. A constant state of being mad. He's lost his good judgment as far as I can see. What I'm saying is that even though I understand he's the one who hired you, he shouldn't be above suspicion."

Nolan put down his pen. "I don't understand."

"Please don't tell my wife I'm proposing any of this, but Julia mentioned your theory—that someone who knew the location of the jewels hired a man to steal them. That the kidnapping was never planned; it just happened. What I'm saying is maybe Gates decided, as punishment for Julia—sorry, for Sarah—as punishment for her wanting to marry Colin, he arranged to get the jewels back. He was the one who hired someone to rob her while she was gone. It was just terribly unfortunate that she came home early."

"But he wasn't at that luncheon. How would he know where the jewels were hidden?"

"I personally told him what went on at that luncheon. I talked to him about his wife's care—sorry, his ex-wife's—and I mentioned it in passing. I thought the sock in the trunk was a humorous detail."

Nolan absorbed this new information. Dutton had known the sock was in a *trunk*. "But if Gates was involved, why would he spend a lot of money to have me find the man responsible? He would know who the man is already."

"Maybe the man has fled with Julia and demanded a ransom and Gates can't find him. Think about it. Maybe Gates—"

"Fled with *Sarah*."

"Sorry, with Sarah, and maybe Gates wants you to find him so he can kill him, or have him killed, before the police find him too and learn that Gates was involved. Did you ever think of that?" The starkness of the charge suddenly stopped the conversation. Dutton slowly pushed away his plate. "I'm just saying it's something to consider." He drank a few more sips of wine. "Personally, I don't think he was involved. No, not at all."

Now a waiter came with the bill on a small silver tray.

"This goes on my wife's account. Marcel, the maître d', he knows how to handle it. Just take this up to Marcel."

Nolan closed the diary and put it in his pocket. "One last question, sir. Are you going to be at the Biltmore much longer?"

"We live at the Biltmore when we're not traveling. Personally, I don't enjoy New York that much anymore, but this is where my wife wants to be, and I want to please her. Personally, I prefer London or Paris."

He tipped up the wine glass to relieve it of the last drop.

The Biltmore cab wrangler

16

Following the Clues

~◦~

A FTER SHAKING HANDS with Dutton in the lobby and watching him disappear onto an elevator, Nolan approached the busy front desk.

Standing in line, he studied the harried young clerk. *New on the job*, he decided, *someone who might be easily intimidated by a detective's badge.* Nolan hoped to convince him to hand over the Duttons' telephone records.

Finally, he moved up to the desk and briefly flashed his badge. Then he asked to see the records.

"I need them quickly. I'm investigating a kidnapping."

"Gosh, a kidnapping. Gosh. Let me think. Uh ... certainly. Let me go get someone."

"Wait. You can't just get the records yourself?"

"No. Just stay right here. The manager is out back."

He disappeared through an office door behind the desk. When he reappeared, he was with the manager—an older, officious-looking man who was not going to be bullied.

"Can I help you? I'm the hotel manager."

"I hope so. I'm looking for phone records for someone."

"Do you have a court order?"

"Uh, not with me. I was hoping—"

"Can I see identification?"

Reluctantly, Nolan took out his badge again. The manager glanced at it and sternly shook his head. "You're a private detective. You're not the police."

"I never said I was the police."

"No one's going to show you any records, friend. You should have known that. Please step out of the line. Other people are waiting."

With the manager's eyes following him, Nolan started to leave the hotel but stopped at the concierge's desk and asked if there was a public phone nearby. He was directed to the gift-shop alcove.

In his leather diary, he found Cochran's number at the station house, deposited a nickel, and got the operator to place the call. Whoever answered went and got Cochran. He was immediately belligerent when Nolan told him who he was.

"Make it quick."

"Is there a way you can get the records of someone's calls while they're staying at a hotel? I know the hotel keeps the records."

"You go to court and get a warrant. Whose records are you talking about?"

"Robert Dutton."

"The girl's father?"

"Stepfather."

"You're trying to tell me you believe her father had her kidnapped? That's what you're telling me?"

"He didn't have her kidnapped. He had her robbed, and the rest was an accident. She came home when she wasn't supposed to and now the robber he hired is ransoming her. At least that's my theory, just something I want to look into."

"Wasn't he out of the country somewhere?"

"He was, but that doesn't mean he couldn't have hired someone to rob her."

"And why in God's name are you looking at him?"

"He doesn't have the money in that family. His wife does. He needs money. He just took his own company into bankruptcy."

"How do you know he doesn't have money? These people earn and lose fortunes all the time. They still have millions."

"For one thing, he took me to lunch and put it on his wife's account."

"That's your proof? His wife paid for lunch?"

"He also said some things during lunch. I'm pretty sure his wife runs that marriage, 'cuz he has no money."

"You're 'pretty sure'? So he didn't say that. You're just guessing."

"He kept saying how he has to let her make all the decisions."

"What decisions?"

"Well, things like, well, she wanted to go steaming down the coast. He hates the ocean, but he let her have her way anyway."

"You ever been married, you fool? That's how most husbands operate, how they get their way in the bedroom. Idiot."

"No. I'm certain this man is broke. He's at her mercy. He needed those jewels. I want to investigate it."

"Your hunch is the girl's own stepfather had her kidnapped."

"Is there a way to get the records or not?"

"I'm not going to insult that poor family with something like this. Don't waste my time, you idiot."

Cochran hung up. Exasperated, Nolan went back to the lobby. He took a chair by the window and surveyed the employees rushing here and there with luggage, flowers, brooms, and dusting feathers.

Bribing an employee to get the telephone records might work. He closed his eyes and gave it some thought. Slipping Cochran a half dollar was one thing. It was a gratuity. Like in a restaurant for good service. To offer an out-and-out bribe to get records illegally was another. It could get him thrown in jail. Besides that, it made him feel dirty. No, all his instincts were against it.

On the front sidewalk, he stood in a drizzle, trying to figure out where to catch a trolley or subway. He began watching the Biltmore's cab wrangler, in his top hat and rain slicker. He had a station by the entrance. A couple exited the hotel with luggage, asked the wrangler for a taxi to the Cunard Line piers. He recorded something in a book on the station's standing desk, then went to the cab line to ask the chauffeurs who would take the fare.

Nolan moved to the desk and leaned against the wall beside it as the wrangler returned.

"You need help, sir?"

Nolan produced his badge. "I'm a private detective. You've probably heard about the kidnapping of the Dutton girl?"

The wrangler nodded and removed his top hat in respect. "Very sad. How long's she been gone?"

"Twenty-one days." Nolan said. "I've been hired by the family to help. There's a man we're looking for."

Nolan always carried handbills with the description of the robber and the stolen jewels. He gave one to the wrangler. Nolan said he was worried the man might try to ransom the jewels by confronting the Duttons at the Biltmore.

"Do you mind if I camp here for a while? Maybe I can help you keep the line moving."

"I pocket the tips though," the wrangler said, winking at him. He turned to the next guest with luggage. "Where are you going, Mr. Clarke?"

"Maxim's Restaurant."

"Horse or horsepower?"

"I'll take a motor," the man said. The wrangler picked up a nub of a pencil from the desk and wrote in the book, a procedure Nolan watched carefully. Then he headed to the cab line.

Nolan turned to the next guest. "Sir, can I ask where you're going and your name?"

With his answer, Nolan took up the pencil and entered the information in the book. After making sure the wrangler was still engaged, he discreetly turned the pages to previous months, looking for Dutton's name. When was Sarah's luncheon? A month before the kidnapping, Julia had said. If Dutton put together this plan, he would have done it in the month between that lunch—when he learned where the jewels were—and the kidnapping. Nolan began with November nineteenth, scanned those pages, then the twentieth, then the twenty-first. There it was. Dutton. Cab to West 26th. What building number, though?

He found the answer on November twenty-seventh and again on the twenty-eighth: 239 West 26th.

In the Tenderloin.

Gun drawn, Nolan approaches the door

17

The Tenderloin

~⌐

Rᴜɴɴɪɴɢ ᴜᴘ ᴛʜᴇ lower middle of Manhattan between Fifth and Eighth Avenues nearly to Central Park, the Tenderloin was, during its heyday in the late 1800s, home to brothels, gambling dens, dance halls, theaters, saloons, and everything else that made it a colorful destination in the evenings. It was also home to the highest concentration of crime and police corruption in the city.

The Tenderloin supposedly got its name this way. City Police Captain "Clubber" Williams, after being transferred into the district in the 1870s, supposedly commented that the bribes he was getting were so much bigger that he could go from eating chuck steak to tenderloin. He also is credited with the comment, "There is more law in the end of a policeman's nightstick than in a decision of the Supreme Court."

Attracting artists, actors, musicians, and bohemians as residents, the Tenderloin had districts within the district, Nolan learned, soon after arriving in the city. The brothels were concentrated on 29th Street, with names like The Star and Garter, The Cremorne, and The Newport. On 28th there was gambling for the rich. On 27th there was gambling for the poor. The music publishers were on Tin Pan Alley, located on one block of 28th Street. On every corner there were saloons, each with a ladies' entrance, as well as nearby hotels that catered to prostitutes and their clients, renting rooms by the hour.

As Nolan walked away from the Biltmore, a plan was forming

in his mind. It was drizzling, and his revolver was at home. He would have to get that first. No, go to the library first to see if Timothy Gates' address in the Tenderloin was the address Dutton repeatedly visited. Then get the revolver.

His heart was pounding as he walked west on 42nd Street toward the New York Public Library, involuntarily breaking into a run at moments. He attempted to work out the possibilities in his mind as he climbed the library's front steps, past the massive statues of lions guarding its door.

Theory one. Dutton and Timothy Gates would meet at Gates' apartment, where they conspired to rob Sarah and split the proceeds. Certainly, they both needed money. However, Dutton was going to be out of the country. Maybe the young man refused to do it himself, so he said he would hire a friend—the blond-haired man—to do it. The crime went awry, and the friend decided to keep the jewels and hold the girl for ransom.

Theory two. Timothy Gates had no part in it. The address 239 West 26th Street belonged to the blond-haired robber, hired solely by Dutton, and it was where the robber and Dutton cooked up the theft. Would he find Sarah tied up and gagged in the apartment?

In the main reading room, Nolan went to a reference librarian, who recommended either voter registration records or the new city directory to find Timothy's address.

In the records room, Nolan went through the district voting records first. He wasted ten minutes looking for "Dutton, Timothy" instead of "Gates, Timothy," but he still found nothing in those records.

He finally found what he wanted in the city directory. His eyes almost skipped over it the first time.

Gates—Timothy, 222 West. 34th St., artist.

So, it was not Gates' address. Dutton hired the blond man to do it, and it was more than likely the blond man's address.

NOLAN STOOD IN the doorway of a Wells Fargo warehouse across the street from the building, a four-story tenement with an iron fire escape on its front. A section had been taken out so that a sign, "Lasell Hat M'F'G. Co.," could be painted over. The persistent drizzle earlier in the day was turning to sleet as temperatures fell and daylight diminished.

As he considered how he would enter, his hand was on his revolver in his pocket, his fingers memorizing its grip and the position of the trigger. He had planned to wait until dusk. Sunset would not be until nearly five o'clock, an hour from now. Better to risk it in the daylight.

He crossed the street, dodging a motor truck. The building's front door was not locked. On the first floor, a woman holding a baby was putting trash in a hallway can.

"Excuse me," he whispered, showing his badge, "did you ever see a well-dressed man, maybe thirty-five, a big mustache, wears fine clothes, come in here? He might've come in several times a couple of months ago."

She said nothing but pointed upstairs.

"Second or third floor?" Nolan asked, again in a whisper.

She held up two fingers and then pointed to the front of the building.

Nolan nodded. She went back inside, and he heard two locks close. As he crept upstairs, he drew the revolver. He knew he could not go to the door, knock, and say he was a detective. The robber might flee out the window, or worse still, injure the girl if she were in there.

At the door, he took a deep breath, listening for noise inside. He heard a cough and what sounded like a wooden match pulled across a striker. He knocked lightly and then heard footsteps coming toward the door. It did not open, but he heard breathing on the other side. He knocked lightly again.

"Who is it?"

Nolan could not tell if it was the voice of a man or a woman.

"A friend of Robert Dutton."

"My sister ain't here."

Nolan had to think about that. "I'm just delivering a message."

"Written?"

"What?"

"Did he write out a note for her?"

"It's a message, uh, a memorized message I'm supposed to give her."

"She's not here. She's at the corner, getting vegetables."

"I can tell you the message and you can tell her. Dutton won't mind."

"Then tell me."

"I don't want to stand in the hallway saying it. It's personal."

A moment passed. Nolan heard a lock click and a chain being slid. The door cracked open only a few inches, and Nolan shoved it hard with his foot, forcing it open and pushing the point of the revolver inside.

There was no blond-haired man. This was a boy, maybe fourteen, maybe Italian, with black hair, holding a rolled cigarette. Taken off guard, he fell back off balance but kept his footing.

"What's going on?" He appeared frantic and frightened. "Please! Please, I didn't do nothing."

"Quiet down," Nolan said. "You know Dutton?"

"I know his name. That's all." The boy backed up, his hands raised defensively as if he were still expecting a bullet. "He and my sister are friends. He comes by. Please don't do nothing."

"That's all? Dutton and your sister are friends?"

"Yes, he takes her to dinner once in a while. He likes her company. I don't even really know him. Please."

They stared across the room at each other.

"Just be quiet a minute." Nolan said, thinking out the situation. "All right. I want you to walk ahead of me into each room. I want to see what's here. And remember, I'm right behind you."

The search proceeded, the boy glancing back periodically, fear in his eyes. When Nolan was satisfied the apartment was empty except for them, he gestured with the revolver for them to return to the front room.

"Look, I don't care about what goes on with your sister and Dutton," Nolan said. "That's none of my business, if dinner is all that's going on."

The boy looked like he was starting to believe he would not be shot. "Then what do you want?"

"It's about Dutton and something else."

"What else."

"Did Dutton ever talk about his daughter?"

"My sister didn't know he was married. Honestly. It was a shock to her. She wouldn't've gone out with him elsewise."

"Did he ever mention a daughter named Sarah?"

"I never talked to him except to answer the door for my sister when he came. He always took her to Delmonico's, then the theater, then he would bring her home. She would bring me what was left over from the restaurant. He liked pork chops, so that's what I got—pork chops."

Nolan tried again to think out the situation. As he did, he heard footsteps coming up the hall stairs. He put the revolver in his pocket and moved out of sight of the hallway door.

"I won't pull this again, if you just let me ask her a few questions," Nolan whispered to the boy, who nodded agreement.

The sister, perhaps twenty-five, had a beautiful dark face beneath jet-black hair. She carried a small bag of groceries and wore a black rain slicker and galoshes.

When she saw Nolan, she asked, "Who're you?"

He took out his badge. "This is nothing to be worried about. I don't even know your name and won't ask it. I just want to ask you a few other questions."

"It's about your friend, Mr. Dutton," the boy said accusingly. "I told you not to go out with him, didn't I?"

"Don't talk to me like that!"

She glared at her brother and then went across the room with her groceries. She deposited them on top of the ice box and took off her slicker and boots, eyeing Nolan as she did. "What is it you want to ask?"

"Robert Dutton. You're friends with him?"

"Yes." At the sink, she put water on a cloth and prepared to wipe off two carrots and a half-dozen apples.

"When was the last time you saw him?"

When she did not immediately answer, the brother, who was a good five inches shorter, grabbed her arm and shook her. "This detective asked you something. Answer him!"

She pushed him away and swung the wet cloth at him. "Did you just grab me? Don't ever grab me, if you know what's good for you."

"The detective and me, we're waiting for an answer."

She charged him, swinging the towel, but Nolan got between them, pushing the boy back. "Calm down."

The sister stamped her foot. "Go to your bedroom and shut up! I don't want to hear nothing from you. Or I'll kick you right out of here."

They stared at each other but he did not move. "Now! I said *right now*."

Glowering, he left. The little brother trying to finally get a hand up on his big sister. He remembered fighting with his older sisters, who always ordered him about like a child. It took him until he was twelve to hold his own, even with the youngest.

Now the sister returned to the sink and vegetables.

"Do you recall the last time you saw him?" Nolan asked.

Glancing at the bedroom door, she whispered, "It was before Christmas."

Nolan whispered as well. "December what? Do you remember the date?"

"A week or so before Christmas. Then he sent me a letter about some trouble in his family and it ended."

"His daughter?"

"You know about that?"

"Did he ever talk about his daughter?"

"No. Honestly, I didn't know he had one until I read it in the papers. It took him a while to even tell me he was married, and when he talked about his family, it was only about his wife. He talked a lot about how unhappy he was. He said he was going to leave her."

She was trying to raise the lid on the ice box, but it was sticking. Nolan did it for her. Trying to be sympathetic, he said, "Didn't you think he might be lying about wanting to leave her?"

She laughed involuntarily. "They all lie about that. First they lie about being married, then you find out and they tell you the second lie. I guess in a way I didn't care. I knew this had developed into a mistake, but I was happy to be out for a night on someone else's nickel. That's how it works in New York. These men, they all hate their wives. And girls make mistakes listening to them."

"So you would go out."

"Yes, we'd go to dinner at the Grand Hotel, then to the theater or to Marie's, the dance hall."

"You didn't go to Delmonico's?"

She clearly realized that he had talked to her brother.

"Sure, sometimes to Delmonico's."

Her suspicions raised, she answered everything Nolan asked after that, giving him little or no information.

"Did he ever talk about his financial situation?"

"Not that I recall."

"Did he say anything to give you the idea he was worried about money?"

She shook her head. "No, not that I recall."

Knowing he would get nothing more of value, he ended the questioning and left. Her last name was written on a mailbox in the downstairs foyer: Carnelli.

THE NEXT MORNING, at the Grand Hotel, after showing his badge to several employees, he found a porter who recalled Dutton and the woman.

"I might know something, yes."

When he did not immediately provide the information, Nolan took out a quarter and offered it to him.

The porter smirked. "That's all?"

"Look, I'm only a private detective, and I get paid what you get paid."

The man took the quarter. "Yes, sometimes he would come in during the afternoon to reserve a room, then he would come back an hour later with the woman you're talking about."

"And they'd eat in the dining room?"

"No. In his room. Sometimes I delivered the trays. I'm no detective but I knew what was going on."

"Would she spend the night?"

"Never. But he didn't either. They would go out before the theaters opened, so I guess that's where'd they'd go. But they would never come back afterward. Yes, I certainly knew what was going on."

"Did a man ever join them, about forty, looked Swedish, five feet six or eight or so?"

The porter shook his head. "Don't recall such a man."

"When was the last time Dutton and the woman were in together? Was it December?"

"No. Yesterday or the day before."

"Are you sure?"

"I'm very sure."

"Can you think which it was, yesterday or the day before? There's a big difference."

"What's this. Sunday? Let's see ...."

The porter paused a little too long to think, so Nolan took out another quarter, showing it to the man but holding on to it.

"It was last night, because Friday they had me scrubbing

down a room where someone died on the sixth floor, so I wouldn't've seen them Friday. It was definitely yesterday."

"Do you recall what time exactly?"

"Let's see. Around dinner, about six."

After I spoke to her, Nolan thought.

"But they didn't get a room," the porter said. "I saw them in the anteroom off the lobby, standing and talking."

The quarter changed hands.

The threatening letter

18

The Black Hand

❧

THE ENVELOPE HAD no stamp. It was addressed only to "John
Nolan" and it found its way into his tenement mailbox
sometime during the night.

Nolan examined it in the hallway as other tenants left on
their way to church. He ripped open the envelope and unfolded
the note inside. The text, with its sloppiness and imperfections,
looked as if it had been printed with a child's block-letter
printing set.

> John Nolan,
>
> You can see we know your name and we know where
> you live. We are warning you that the worst harm will
> come to you if you keep searching for the man you tried
> to grab in Newark. He is our friend and associate. If you
> do not stop, we have a shot gun prepared for you, YOU
> DOG!!! What a fine feast for the rats your carcass will
> make when we are done!!! Do what we say or else it will
> be your skin!!!
>
> Stop looking for the Newark man!!!
>
> THE BLACK HAND

At the bottom of the page were a roughly drawn black dagger,
black skull, and black hand.

* * *

TIERNEY SAT ON the edge of his desk as he read the letter. When he finished, he snorted his disgust.

"Stupid letter. 'A fine feast for the rats'? That supposed to scare you?"

"Well, it does. What do I do?"

"I wouldn't do nothing. Just look both ways when you come out of your building. Maybe take out some life insurance for the benefit of your fiancée."

Tierney picked up the phone and looked over at Nolan. "I know a man'll sell you a policy cheap. I'll call him, if you're interested."

Nolan could only shake his head.

Tierney laughed as he put down the phone and handed back the letter. "I'm kidding you, Cousin. You know anything about the Black Hand?"

"What everyone knows," Nolan said.

"Everyone knows nothing. I had to deal with these letters on the force. You know who you can blame for this?"

"Who?"

"Mr. Enrico Caruso."

He told the story of how in 1910 the famed tenor received a letter threatening death unless money was paid. It was signed by the Black Hand, the secret Italian organization of terror. Caruso paid it, nearly two thousand dollars, and the fact became well known in the underground. Within a week, Caruso was in receipt of a stack of similar Black Hand letters, all demanding money.

"And he never stops getting them. Now blackmail by the Black Hand is one of the city's biggest industries. Everyone what's got any money gets these letters. It's disrespectful if you're rich and you don't."

"Mine isn't about money, though."

"Let's see it again." Tierney took back the letter and studied it. "The way yours reads, nothing's gonna happen unless they're convinced you're still going after the man in Newark. So you have a few days before they're convinced of anything, Cousin. But listen, far as I know there isn't no Black Hand in this country. It doesn't exist. All it is is a name what gives fools a simple way to extort money out of someone. It's a scare thing."

Tierney handed back the letter. Nolan sighed as he reread it. "So you had to deal with a lot of these?"

"I did, Cousin."

"How often did they carry through with their threats?"

"Not often. Most of the letters were just that, threats."

"What's 'most' mean?"

"Most means most."

"Does it mean fifty-one out of a hundred of these are nothing or does it mean ninety-nine out of a hundred are nothing?"

"In between somewhere."

"Eighty-five?"

"Maybe."

"Eighty?"

"You gotta stop those accounting classes, Cousin."

"Let's say eighty. Four out of five times, it's nothing. But one out of five times, they blow up your house, kill your wife and children and your cat because you don't pay them the thousand dollars."

"If you're J.P. Morgan, it ain't a thousand. I know. I read the letters. Besides, my guess is there are no Black Handers behind this. My guess is the man you beat up in Newark cooked this up to scare you."

LATELY, WHEN THE Frenchman could not sleep at night, he would wander the apartment whispering to himself, believing that by speaking softly he was being courteous to Nolan as he tried to sleep. It would still keep Nolan awake unless he packed his ears with cotton.

And lately, the Italian family that lived on the other side of Nolan's bedroom wall, whose income depended on home piecework for the garment trade, would run their sewing machine at all hours of the night.

Now the Black Hand letter weighed on him as well, making sleep on this night nearly impossible.

Once, when he was nine years old, he had hired out for two days to a neighbor as a live scarecrow to guard the man's potato vines when he went to Dublin for his daughter's wedding. Coming home in the evening, Nolan took a shortcut through the bed of a pond that he believed to be dry. However, in the fading daylight, he failed to see the darker ground of a huge mud hole and walked into it.

After several steps, his shoes began to sink, and feeling no bottom to the mud, he panicked. He tried yanking his legs free, but the struggling only made him sink faster. When he had sunk to mid-thigh, he was terrified. Unable to think of a way out, he realized he might be pulled in to his death.

When he was nearly waist-deep, out of instinct and nothing else, he leaned backward and lay flat on the mud, arms outstretched. This stopped his sinking. He tried calling out, but his voice was weak and the pond was isolated at the far end of a fallow field where no one could possibly hear him.

Over the next twenty minutes, instinct continued to guide him. Still lying on his back, he slowly eased one leg out, then the other. Still lying flat, he was able to wriggle backward to firmer ground on the edge of the hole. When he finally did escape, his shoes lost and his body caked in mud, he broke down and cried.

His lasting memory of the experience was of the sharp fear he felt when he realized he was in so deep that he might not be able to extricate himself. That he did escape seemed to him a miracle. ("God wants you for something besides plugging up a mud hole," his father told him.)

Now, as the Frenchman passed his door, muttering under his breath, and as the sewing machine whined in the next apartment, Nolan thought of the Black Hand letter and felt that same sickening fear.

HE FOUND ANOTHER tenement flat in the *Tribune*'s classifieds. "273 115th St., apartment, water, heat, 5 rooms." When he went to see it, what he liked was that it was on the top floor, had no elevator, and would be difficult to reach. Also, the flat had a strong oak door.

However, it had two bedrooms, so he needed a roommate. At the direction of Tierney, he went to police headquarters and asked if any new patrolmen were looking for inexpensive housing. Indeed, there were more than a dozen living with their parents who wanted to be out now that they had positions in the department.

Within a day, Nolan informed the Frenchman of his problem and notified the landlord they were both moving out, the Frenchman to live with his sister in Brooklyn. In the new building, there was nothing on the mailbox to identify Nolan or the police recruit, and Nolan had added two extra bolt locks to the heavy entry door of the apartment.

The next night, as the new roommates prepared to sit down to a dinner of boiled pork and potatoes, they removed their suit coats nearly simultaneously to reveal that both were wearing holstered revolvers. They looked from one to the other, laughed heartily, and sat down to eat, leaving the guns right where they were.

Timothy Gates

19

The Painter

❧

"I'M LOOKING FOR Timothy Gates. He's an artist."

"We're all artists. What's he? Landscapes or portraits?"
Nolan shrugged.

"If you figure it out, the portrait people are in that corner. They have their own grievances with the academy."

The room at the Grand Union Hotel was crowded with men and a few women. The men were mostly bearded, mostly standing in small groups, mostly smoking pipes or cigarettes so that the collective haze of smoke made breathing a chore.

Nolan had been to Gates' apartment in the Tenderloin each of the last three mornings without finding him home. Each time, he left his card with the agency telephone number on it and versions of the same note.

Dear Timothy,

In the matter of the kidnapping of your sister I've been hired by your family to investigate the crime. I'm hoping to interview you about your memory of things your sister may have said prior to the crime regarding friends or others who were inside her apartment in the weeks before she was taken.

When can I call on you?

With great sympathy for your suffering,
John Nolan

He had received no call or other communication in response. This morning, though, he had returned to the address—a tenement more tumbledown than his own, with a missing stair banister and no lights in any hallway—and found a scrawled note pinned to Gates' apartment door: *Meet at the Union Hotel at noon.*

Nolan guessed the message was not intended for him. With several lessons behind him, he had begun driving on city streets, so he took the agency Ford to the hotel on 41st Street. At the desk, he learned that a group of painters was scheduled to meet with an official of the National Academy of Design in a second-floor banquet room at noon.

Nolan had seen Timothy Gates only once, from a distance at the special Mass. He could not say a single thing about his appearance, except that he had no beard and appeared to be in his twenties.

Now Nolan waded into another group that had at least one clean-shaven member. "I'm looking for Timothy Gates. He's one of the artists."

Initially, no one acknowledged they were Gates, but as he turned to move on to the next group, a young man with no beard took hold of his arm.

"Are you from the academy?"

"No, I'm not."

"If I see Timothy, what's he done? Is it bills he owes?"

Nolan knew this was Timothy. "No, nothing like that."

"Then what is it?"

"It's, uh, it's a family matter."

Hearing the word "family," the young man's expression turned sour and he let go of Nolan's arm. "If I see him, I'll tell him you're looking for him."

Sensing that Gates was going to be unwilling to talk to him, he moved to the side of the room to plan another approach.

The purpose of the meeting, it turned out, was to complain to the academy official about the choice of works displayed at the winter exhibition. The official, who had arrived late, stood by the door without removing his greatcoat.

"Every year," said the first man to address him, "you favor the artists of past generations, not the new artists doing new things."

"We favor the people whose work the public wants to see."

"And why do they want to see it? Because that's the only work you hang, so it's the only work they know anything about."

Cheers broke out and impassioned speeches followed. To Nolan, the most interesting statement was made by a painter whose submissions had been turned down. The painter said he had borrowed a work by Matisse owned by his family and submitted that, along with two works of his own. All had been rejected.

"Am I to respect your jurors after that? They cannot even recognize a Matisse, and his name was right on the canvas."

Gates spoke only once during the hour the meeting lasted.

"My charge is this," he said. "And I'm not the only one this happened to. I had a painting accepted by the jury, but was notified it would not be hung because wall space had run out. Yet, I know of nearly twenty painters who had at least two paintings displayed. Why could not one of their spaces be given to me and others like me?"

"It's the works that are given priority for wall space, not the painter," said the academy official. "If one painter had all the best works, he would have gotten all the wall space."

Gates threw up his hands and groaned.

More individual complaints followed—the favoring of oils over watercolors, of large canvases over small, of male artists over females. However, at one o'clock, the academy official, who had remained by the door the entire time, pulled out his pocket watch and raised it for all to see.

"We love our New York artists," he said and abruptly left.

The strangeness of his exit seemed to leave everyone momentarily stunned. Then, slowly, the crowd began moving toward the door. Nolan intercepted Gates.

"Timothy, if you don't answer my questions, I promise you police will be right behind me with a warrant. You need to talk to me first, for your own protection."

Startled by this, Gates stepped out of the flow of the crowd and stood by a wall. "What questions? What questions are you talking about?" He was clearly upset. As Nolan drew out his diary, Gates seemed to change his mind. Pushing him away, he said, "No. I don't see why I have to answer any questions at all. In fact, I have to leave."

"Please, Timothy, I can take you to lunch if you like. I think I saw a restaurant right next to the hotel."

Gates was silent for a moment, thinking.

"Timothy, your family hired me to help. Please."

"You'll pay for it?"

"For lunch, yes. Also, I've got a motor in case you need a ride somewhere after."

"But what questions? What do the police want to talk to me for?"

THE RESTAURANT NOLAN had seen turned out to be a crowded saloon with a "businessman's lunch" of Hungarian goulash, pie, and coffee for twenty-five cents. They took their food to a back room and found a table by the kitchen. Within a minute of sitting down, Gates had nearly cleaned his bowl of goulash.

"I just want to ask you about the kidnapping—the same questions you'll hear from the police detectives," Nolan said, opening his diary. "So you can prepare your answers. Just be honest, and we'll see how we can present this to them in the best light."

Nolan hoped his little fiction would coax out the truth.

"Why would I want to present this any way at all?" Gates said. "I did nothing, so the facts are good enough."

"Sometimes it's how things look, not how they are."

"Are you saying the police actually think I'm involved in this? Me?"

"The police think someone who knew Sarah is involved, so they're not looking at anyone in particular. They're looking at everyone. So don't take it personal. But first, when was the last time you talked to anyone in your family?"

"Haven't you heard? They shun me."

"So you haven't talked to them recently."

"Not since the Mass for Sarah."

"One thing the police are going to ask about is the farm you went to in Albany for your cocaine problem."

"Which is where I was when it happened. The police up there checked it, I was told. But it wasn't for cocaine. I can't afford cocaine anymore. It was for alcohol. Also, what do you think about me ordering a second bowl of goulash?"

"Go ahead. I'll pay for it. Yes, the Albany police did check it, but I talked to the farm administrator and, well, there's a problem."

"What problem?"

"The problem is that, yes, he told police you were there all weekend. But when I spoke to him, he admitted you were there for a treatment Friday night and then for one on Monday morning, so he assumed you didn't go anywhere in between. "

"I didn't." Gates caught the eye of a busboy. "Listen, could someone bring me another bowl of goulash?"

"But the police might hear that and think you could have made the drive down from Albany Saturday morning."

"I don't drive and I don't have an automobile."

"You've never driven?"

"I've taken my father's motor around our place in White Plains. Not on the roads, though."

"Then you've driven is what the police will say."

"Does my father think I had some part in this?"

"Not at all. He's trying to protect you. He doesn't want to lose another child."

"He said that?"

"That's what I took his meaning to be." Nolan liked that fiction. He turned pages in his diary. "I need to ask you about the things you did the Saturday your sister was kidnapped."

"Have you ever spent time in a sanitarium? You lose track of what day it is, what hour, whether it's day or night. Hot baths, steam rooms, dark rooms, not to mention the tonics and injections. I heard one place shoots horse blood into you. There *is* no sense of time in a sanitarium. I can't tell you anything about that Saturday other than, according to sanitarium records, I apparently existed on Earth that day."

"All right, can you tell me who your friends were at the farm?"

"No one's still up there. They've all been paroled too."

"Who were your friends, though? Can you describe them, if you can't remember their names?"

Gates shook his head as the bowl of goulash was delivered. He eagerly raised his spoon. "I didn't have any friends there."

"The administrator said you seemed to enjoy talking with a man who may have been from Sweden or Holland."

"He wasn't from Sweden. He was from Pennsylvania. He was born in Pennsylvania."

"Maybe he was of Dutch extraction, though. Did he have blond or light-brown hair? A lot of them do."

"He may have. I don't recall."

"It's important."

"I don't recall. You ask people the color of the hair or eyes of someone they just met, how many can recall that? Men can't. Maybe a few women can."

"But you were friends with this man."

"No. We talked a couple of times about Bellevue. He'd been in there too."

"Here in the city?"

"Yeah, that Bellevue. I spent a few days in the rounders' ward there and I don't ever want to go back."

"Do you remember this man's name?"

"He never told me."

"In the long drive down from Albany, he didn't mention his name, maybe his first name?" Nolan spoke casually and quickly, meaning it as a trap.

Gates stopped eating and stared at him with agitation. "What kind of damn question is that?" Now he was upset.

"Calm down, Timothy. It's the kind of thing the police might ask to trick you. I had to see if you might fall into that kind of trap. You didn't, though. Good for you. All right. Did you mention your sister's jewels to this man?"

"You mean did he get it into his head to skip the bath treatments and drive down to New York himself to steal her jewels and kidnap her?" He laughed. "No, I never mentioned the jewels. Only Bellevue. You can get his name from the farm administrator, I'm sure. Go find him in Pennsylvania and see if he's got Sarah and is living high on those jewels, why don't you."

He had finished the goulash and dug into the lemon meringue pie.

"I have to ask these things, Timothy. I'm sorry. Another question. When was the last time you saw your sister before the kidnapping?"

Wary now, Gates sipped his coffee. "A few weeks before. She invited me over to lunch."

"Did she talk about her jewels at all? Did she show them to you? You want my pie, go ahead. Take it."

He did. "The jewels never came up. Except in one way. I hoped she might sell one of the pieces and sponsor me as a painter. I think she would've ... if she hadn't been kidnapped."

"Did she show you the jewels? It's something the police will ask."

"No."

"Did she tell you where she kept them?"

"No."

"You're sure?"

"I'm sure."

"Was there anyone else at the lunch besides you and Sarah?"

"How do you know the police will ask any of this?"

Nolan had to think fast. "I heard they plan to go back to everyone who knows Sarah and ask harder questions the second time around. I've been hired by your father to help you with the answers .... Was anyone else at the lunch?"

Gates seemed to accept the invented explanation. "I don't remember and I don't care."

"Timothy. Think. Police will care. Wasn't Julia there, maybe?"

"You talked to her?"

"Not yet. I'll get to her later. I was just guessing."

"Yes, I suppose she was there. But if you talk to her, she's going to tell you they blackmailed me to go upstate to the farm, her and my sister and my mother. It's not true. I meant to go anyway because I let my drinking get out of hand, I admit."

"What about the jewels? You say they never came up?"

"As I recall."

"Did they or didn't they come up?"

"I already told you!" He spoke loudly enough that other patrons turned. "Not that I recall. Maybe Julia'll give you a different story."

"Where do you think Sarah kept her jewels, the ones your father gave her?"

"Why would the police ask that? Don't they already know?"

"They'll want to know if you knew."

"They think I stole my own sister's jewels and then kidnapped her?" He stared at Nolan in disbelief. "My *own* sister?"

"They might think it was an accident, that you went there to take them, and she came home unexpectedly, so your plan changed."

"I could have robbed a hundred other people who had money. I've been in the houses of the Vanderbilts, the Schwabs, the Carnegies. Thousand-dollar things are everywhere in those homes. Everywhere."

"But wasn't the hiding place for those jewels talked about during the lunch? "

"I don't recall." Gates rose. "Listen, I have to go. I don't want a ride. I'll walk."

"You sure you don't recall?"

Gates leaned over the table until he was nose to nose with Nolan.

"I don't recall because I ... was ... drunk!"

"You were drunk?"

"To have to go to a lunch with my mother and sisters and be forced to listen to the shit they think about me, yes, I got very drunk first."

With that, he left.

Colin Flannery

20

The Stevedore

❧

TUESDAY NIGHT INTO early Wednesday, a ferocious storm swept in from the Atlantic, leaving nearly a foot of snow from Philadelphia to Boston.

At sea, ships had to contend with wind gusts of hurricane force that created thirty-foot waves. Several straggled into port the following day covered with ice, but they were kept at anchor off Sandy Hook. The berths along lower Manhattan were fully occupied by ships that had not been able to leave during the storm.

Nolan was set to interview Colin Flannery on the man's day off, Wednesday, but arriving at his boarding house on 44th Street, he learned from another tenant that Flannery had been offered double wages to help unload one of the distressed liners coming into its berth at Chelsea Piers.

Nolan made his way to the docks as city crews worked to clear streets and sidewalks of snow. He found Flannery in a baggage shed at the foot of the pier at West 22nd Street with a gang of other longshoremen, all waiting for the Cunard liner to arrive. When Nolan opened the door, the half-dozen men, all smoking, looked up in silence.

"Is Colin Flannery in here?"

"Who're you?"

Nolan recognized the questioner as Flannery despite the wool cap that covered his red hair.

"John Nolan. You said we could talk this afternoon."

"Fellows, this man is a detective. Is this someone we want to allow into our private Irish cathedral?"

Two instantly got up to leave.

"I'm a private detective," Nolan told them as they passed. "I'm not with the police." They still pushed around him and out the door.

The shed stored unclaimed trunks and suitcases as well as the hooks and hand trucks used by the stevedores. Mainly, it was the smoking lounge for idle longshoremen.

Flannery moved over on the trunk to give him room to sit down. "I seen you at Sarah's Mass. Correct?"

"You did," Nolan said. "I didn't know who you were at the time."

"Well, get down to it. This ship's in trouble and it's supposed to swing in soon. What is it you want to ask?"

"What happened to the ship?"

"Got caught in the storm. A wave came over the deck and swept three men out to sea. Crushed the bridge too."

Nolan took out his diary as the shed's door opened. A roughly dressed man, appearing to be Italian and a longshoreman, looked in and was met with steely gazes and silence. The man said nothing and backed out the door, closing it again. The four seated men, including Flannery, turned to each other and smiled.

"You need to know," Nolan said. "I was hired by the family to help find the kidnapper."

"I hear the longer a kidnapping goes, the less chance it will come out well. What's it been? Almost a month she's been gone?"

"That may be, but I'm hearing the police are going to do a second round of interviews with everyone who knew Sarah. They're out to find someone to arrest, guilty or not. So Captain Gates wants me to help you get through—"

"The captain told you to talk to me in particular?"

"Yes. He wants—"

Now the door opened again and another man, also appearing Italian, looked in. Met with the same belligerent looks, he left without a word.

"He wants me to help you formulate your answers for the police so that you're not framed up. He doesn't want any trouble for you."

"He said that? He doesn't want any trouble for me?"

"That's what I took his intent to be, yes. He wants no more trouble for anyone in the family and he thought I could help in that regard." Flannery seemed to accept this as the truth. "If you don't mind, can we talk in private?"

Flannery sighed, reluctantly rose from the trunk, and picked up his tobacco pouch. Nolan followed him outside where Flannery leaned against a fence and relit his pipe. Out in the channel, through a fog, a liner was slowly making a wide turn into the berth, a pair of tugboats guiding its bow.

Nolan opened his diary. "The main thing here is that you tell me the truth," he said. "And if anything seems like it could be made into something by the police, we can think of another way to present it. But you have to tell me the truth as you remember it."

"Do you know, standing here, I'm not getting paid a thing? Not until that steamer docks does the time clock start. In England, they get a daily wage, no matter if they're standing around waiting or not." He paused to draw on his pipe. "I'll bet you're getting paid by the day. What's a detective earn?"

"Not much. Look, I saw the notes the police detectives had on you. There's something I need to ask about because the police just became aware of it."

Flannery looked concerned. "What?"

"Your temper."

"Everyone has a temper."

"You show yours more than others. There's an arrest record on file for you. You got into a fight that sent a man to the hospital."

"He would've sent me to the hospital if I didn't send him first."

"There's three other arrest records of brawls you were in."

"I never went to jail for those, and in the first one you mentioned, they suspended it because the man whose head I cracked was wanted for murder in New Jersey. They must've felt I did the state of New York a great service."

"There's something else. A woman in Sarah's building said she heard you and Sarah arguing more than once."

"What woman? The witch next door?"

"I don't know who, but she claims these arguments sometimes went on quite a while."

"Let me tell you about Sarah. She's a woman who, if she has an opinion, you cannot change it. Yes, we argued, but if you could've heard what these arguments were about, the side she was arguing for, you would have been in my corner. In fact, I wish you could have been standing there in my corner. You would have pinned a medal on me for trying to reason with her."

Nolan searched his diary again. "All right, let me ask you about Proctor's Theatre. You were supposed to meet Sarah at the ticket window at seven p.m."

"Of course, she didn't show and now we know why. So I went in anyway."

"Why didn't you just walk up the street to her apartment to get her?"

"I was mad at her for not being on time. I'd already paid my money, so I decided to go in. I gave my stub to the police, if you don't believe me. They have it, so go talk to them."

"You go to a lot of vaudeville?"

"All the time. Whenever I can."

"When the vaudeville ended, why didn't you go see Sarah?"

"I told police. She didn't like me showing up at her door late in the evening because she thought it injured her reputation with the witches in that building."

"How late did the show end?"

"I didn't look at my watch, but her rule was I should only come by in daylight, and obviously it was dark when the show got out. I told police that."

"All right. Another thing the police will ask about is the jewels, the ones Gates gave Sarah."

"I don't have them or I wouldn't be standing here working for an hourly wage. Seriously, what do detectives get paid? Is it something I could do?"

"Anyone could do this so you get paid nothing. But the jewels. Were they taken from a trunk in a closet?"

Flannery snickered. "From a *sock* in a trunk in a closet."

"Do you recall how many people knew that? Did Sarah tell some of her friends they were in the sock?"

"She didn't really have friends, not close ones, except her sister. And me."

"Who do you think knew they were in the sock?"

Flannery considered this, drawing on his pipe. "I know she

talked about it during a lunch she put on a few weeks before the robbery. I mentioned how stubborn that girl is. This was quite the example. Everyone at that lunch .... Do you want to know who was there?"

"I think I already know."

Flannery turned to him. "So you've already talked to others in the family."

"A couple, yes."

"What did they have to say about me? Let me guess."

"They didn't say anything against you, Colin."

"Julia didn't utter an unkind word?"

When Nolan was silent, Flannery smiled and then looked out into the channel at the approaching liner, turning slowly toward its berth.

"At that lunch, everyone tried to talk her into moving those jewels into a bank," Flannery said. "She wouldn't hear of it. I pleaded with her and look what happened."

"Well, my theory is that someone who knew where those jewels were set up that robbery," Nolan said. "Sarah walked in before the robber finished and that was her misfortune. If you were the detective, who at that lunch would you be looking at?"

Flannery took a long moment to consider this. One of the tugs blew its whistle several short blasts. "Here's the name that would top my list, and he wasn't even at the lunch. Gates. Captain Gates. And despite his change of heart about me—if you're telling me the truth—I don't like him. When he found out Sarah was planning to marry me, he went around to see her. I wasn't there, but she told me about it. He wrung her arm so bad it nearly broke her wrist. He believed I wanted the marriage because I wanted her money, which is just not true. Did you know Sarah is the one who asked *me* to get married? She loved me, and Gates was ready—by the way, I loved her too—Gates was ready to disown her. Maybe he set up that robbery to take back the fortune he gave her and will have to live with the consequences. He'd top my list, if I was the detective."

The other stevedores exited the shed to await the liner's imminent arrival, its bow having finally straightened out to be in line with the pier.

"So, Mr. Nolan, you haven't answered my question."

"What's that?"

"What do you detectives earn?"

Fifteen minutes later, sitting on an uptown trolley, Nolan added one more note to his diary.

> Never asked anything about the search for the kidnapper. WHY? If Sheenagh was kidnapped, finding her and the man who did it would be all I would think about. His life ruined by this man.

Times Square

21

The Report to Gates

∿

Tribune editorial

CONTROL OF CRIME

It is inspiring to hear of the many improvements in the operation of the police department brought about by Commissioner Woods, an able and fierce reformer, if there ever was one.

However, several of the most heinous crimes committed in our city in recent months continue to go unsolved. One in particular is the kidnapping of Miss Sarah Dutton in December, abducted from her own home and still not found.

If you should think we are singling out this case because the victim was a wealthy and prominent citizen, you would be wrong. It is because it was a widely publicized case, with all elements of the city, and many elements beyond the city, hearing about it. When such an infamous crime cannot be solved, it is dispiriting to the mass of New Yorkers and gives the impression, here and elsewhere, that we cannot properly police our city and that it is an unsafe place in which to live.

* * *

"WHAT'S THIS ITEM? The forty-four cents. Subway fare?" Gates turned the receipt toward Nolan and pointed.

"Gasoline," Nolan said. "I'm driving a motor now. Instead of four pawnshops a day, I can reach nearly eight."

He sat across the massive desk from Gates in his office on Times Square as Gates studied Nolan's weekly expense sheet. They had agreed that Nolan would call Gates every other day with a progress report and meet with him weekly to give him an expense report.

Nolan worried he had seen the *Tribune* editorial that morning and would blame him for not yet finding Sarah and her kidnapper. It was now January fourteenth, and he had been on the case nearly three weeks.

Gates continued to express the belief that the jewels offered the best chance of finding the kidnapper, that they would show up in one of the pawnshops in or around the city. Nolan was therefore under orders to spend much of his week visiting them, sacrificing time he could spend investigating the case in other ways. At least that was the argument Nolan would present in his defense if Gates had seen the editorial and decided he was to blame.

Gates mentioned Sarah less and less when they talked, as if he was giving up hope she was alive but was resolved to see the situation through.

Also in the *Tribune* that morning was the story of an Italian importer whose three-year-old son had been kidnapped five weeks earlier from his store on Broome Street in Manhattan. A $10,000 ransom was demanded "or your boy will be cut up into pieces and sent to you in a jar." The importer said he did not have $10,000 in all the world and could not pay. The police detective on the case was quoted as saying, "Unfortunately, once a couple of weeks go by, there's little chance this will end well." Nolan hoped Gates had not seen this article either.

"What's gasoline cost these days?" Gates asked. "I got a man who drives me, so he fills it, not me."

"Where I buy it, about fourteen cents a gallon," Nolan said. "Sir, uh, something's come up I need to talk to you about."

Gates was still examining the sheet. "Three gasoline fillings in a week. Is that a lot? I don't know nothing about these new models."

"Not a lot for a Ford runabout. Sir, I have some sensitive information you need to hear."

"I'm listening .... Hold on, what's this?" He was still holding the envelope Nolan had handed him containing the expense sheet. Shaking it, he heard coins jangle.

"The change left from the expense money you gave me."

Gates put down the sheet and leaned back in the chair. "John, your honesty makes me nervous. Relax about things. No one's going to fire you. From now on, if I give you ten dollars advance expenses, don't come back with any left over. If you want, use your wits and find a creative method to keep as much of it as you can for yourself. You're still one of the cheapest men on my payroll."

"Yes, sir. Thank you very much." Gates had not seen the editorial, he was sure.

"Now. What information? Oh, before I forget, the suffragettes will march up Fifth Saturday morning. You heard about that?"

"No, sir."

"It's day after tomorrow. Julia wants to watch it from the sidewalk and asks if you can accompany her."

"Accompany her?"

"As her bodyguard. I don't think it's needed, but she seems to fear the crowds. She asked, so I said yes. Talk to my girl outside for the details. Now. What information is it you want to give me?"

"First, could I ask that whatever I tell you, could you please not pass it on to Detective Cochran?"

"Why not?"

"To be honest, I don't like him, and I think he's, well, I think he's a fool. I'm trying to work at this quietly, staying in the shadows so as not to alert anyone I'm investigating. But Cochran is as heavy-handed as you can get. He'll mess it up."

Gates laughed. "Cochran is out then. So this information, what is it?"

Nolan sighed. "I'm sorry to say it involves your wife, your ex-wife."

"Go ahead."

"I've been trying to question her for the past week, but she doesn't leave her room at the Biltmore. I talked to the doctor who has been coming in every other day to check on her, and he's worried."

"Go ahead."

"Apparently, she drinks all day, and he took away some bichloride of mercury tablets from her yesterday. He doesn't know how she got them."

"Go ahead."

"Bichloride of mercury. It's what people use—"

"To commit suicide."

"Yes, sir."

Gates sighed and then stood and walked to his window that looked out on Times Square. "I already knew all this, but thank you for telling me."

"There's something else, sir."

"What's that?"

"It involves Dutton ... Mr. Dutton."

"You're going to tell me the man is bankrupt. I knew that too. That's the only thing that's put a smile on my face during all this."

"Well, yes, he is bankrupt, but I found out, well ...." Nolan hesitated. "Sir, if I give you information about Dutton that makes your wife unhappy ... it concerns me if you tell her, in her state of mind."

"That's my concern. Not yours."

"To be honest, sir, I heard you bear a grudge against your wife."

Gates spun around, anger flashing in his eyes. "You mean will I deliberately give my ex-wife this terrible news you've got to make her more miserable than she already is? Out of spite?"

Gates' tone scared Nolan, who did not respond.

"Is that what you're asking me?"

"I ... uh ...."

"So if I say yes, I'm going to tell the woman, then you're not going to give me this information? You're going to withhold it?"

Again, Gates spoke with such hostility that Nolan kept quiet.

"First, dammit, I'm paying you. You work for me. Understand? You don't determine what information I get and don't get. If I pay you to find this, you damn well tell me what it is. Understand?"

"Yes, sir. Sorry."

Gates turned back to the window on the square, muttering to himself.

"It's bad enough with my daughter and what's happened.

Now my ex-wife and her problems ...." His voice trailed off. "Just tell me what you've got, for God's sake."

"Sir, I've looked into Mr. Dutton and he has a woman what seems to be his mistress in the Tenderloin."

For a moment, Gates was silent, staring out the window. "So what?"

His reaction confused Nolan.

"What this man does," Gates said, "is his business if it has nothing to do with the kidnapping."

"Sir, it may have something to do with it."

Gates turned to face Nolan again. "Go ahead."

"Mr. Dutton has no money. Your wife gives him all his funds, like an allowance. And one line of investigation is whether someone who knew where the jewels were, which he did, someone who needed money, which he did, hired a man to steal them. Then the robbery went bad when your daughter came home unexpected. And now, maybe this individual who set up the robbery is involved in the kidnapping. Maybe he knows where Sarah is being held. That's just one thing I have to investigate."

Gates sat at his desk and sighed heavily.

"How do you know Dutton knew where the jewels I gave Sarah were?"

"She told him and he told me she did."

"Then Dutton is behind this. Correct? Then, damn, let's go after him."

"Sir, other people also knew where the jewels were."

"How many?"

"I don't know yet, but several."

Gates absorbed the news. "Anything more?"

"I did some investigating of the woman Dutton was seeing in the Tenderloin. She has two brothers who've been in Sing Sing upstate for two years. They were convicted of several robberies, including a break-in of a residence belonging to one of the Astor grandsons. They took valuables, including a gold mantel clock, and tried to pawn it. That's when they got caught."

A long silence followed. Nolan was disturbed by Gates' stare. It was as if he were looking right through him, unaware of his presence in the room.

Finally, Gates snapped back to the present. "John, I'm sorry

I yelled at you. This is good work. Indeed, very good. If you come across the editorial in the *Tribune* this morning, just ignore it. I still have faith in you to solve this. Let me know if you find anything more about Dutton."

"Sir, thank you."

"And don't worry about my ex-wife. She's not going to be told, not at the moment. At least I have that much integrity."

A newspaper from home

22

A Letter Home

∾∾

January 15, 1915

Dearest Sheenagh,

I received your letter of Jan. 3 and thank you for that and the *Independent* but I was able to read that very copy two weeks ago. The steamships bring it over and I discovered the libraries here put it out so save the stamps from now on. The paper has certainly not backed off from its war attitude.

I had not heard about Brendan O'Malley tho. Very sad. But I would of picked him as someone who wanted to fight and it didn't matter for who. He would of fought for the Germans if they asked him nicely. He was that sort.

The war news is not good tho. As you said, more ships are sunk everyday by the Germans. But as I read it, the passenger ships still get through if they are flying the American colors or carrying many Americans. When you get ready to cross, the one thing we must make sure of is it's got a few rich Americans in first class.

Concerning your list of ships out of Liverpool next month, you choose. Whatever one you pick I will be here on this end when you land. I promise.

You asked about my kidnapping case. The news is not good there either. It's been more than three weeks the girl has been missing and the chances she is alive are growing slimmer every day. It would seem anyone of the five million people in New York City could have been the man who kidnapped her, if you believe the police or Sean. But I'm convinced the man was hired by someone else who knew exactly where the jewels were in the girl's apartment which brings the list of the suspects down to only a small number. At least that is my best theory and the one I am pursuing. But I'm never sure of anything. Everything comes down to betting odds. In this case the stepfather of the girl—a man named Dutton—started out the betting favorite on the board because I found out he has a mistress who he takes to entertainments around the city and he has no money of his own anymore. His wife, the girl's natural mother, has all the money. I found out today Dutton's bank account is overdrawn. The man what's paying me is the girl's natural father. I think I mentioned Captain Gates in a previous letter. He also has a horse in this race. He didn't like the man his daughter wanted to marry who he thought was only interested in her money. Did he hire someone to steal back the jewels which he gave her as a gift? I don't know, but it's possible. As I say, everything is only odds. The brother of the kidnapped girl who is a poor artist is also on the betting board. Also the girl's fiancé who has a terrible temper.

Here are the latest figures on my savings. $348. Captain Gates now gives me extra each week for expenses that I don't have to tell Sean about. Bless him for that.

Also you asked about church. I'm happy to report my soul has been replenished by a visit to St. Patrick's Cathedral, which is the most famous Catholic church in New York. Enclosed is a postcard showing the church. When you arrive it is the first Mass we will attend.

That's all for tonight. As always, I miss you terribly.

Love and love and more love,

Your John

Rain falls on Fifth Avenue

23

The Suffragettes

❧

IN THE DAYS prior to the suffragettes' march, one minister in the city warned that the procession was evidence of "an advanced stage of general godlessness." Women were growing arrogant and prideful in their quest for the vote.

Nevertheless, the march was expected to draw a large, appreciative crowd, and two precinct policemen were stationed on every block along Fifth Avenue, from Herald Square to Central Park. However, a mix of rain and sleet began to fall before dawn, and the turnout of women willing to tramp in puddles of ice was poor.

At nine a.m., Nolan found Julia Gates at the corner of Fifth Avenue and 52nd Street, holding a large black umbrella. Inexplicably, she wore no overcoat, only a pink spring dress and a broad-brimmed hat ringed with flowers.

"I wanted to give this march some optimistic color," she told him. "My apartment is right around the corner, if I need a coat."

Busloads of women had been expected to turn up for the march, from New Jersey and Long Island, but there were currently no buses in sight.

"You didn't bring an umbrella?" she asked Nolan. With the temperatures warming, the sleet had turned to rain.

"It would slow me down if there's trouble," he said.

"You'd rather get drenched?"

He looked at the skies. "This is more a drizzle than a drenching. I can stand that."

"It doesn't make me look very respectable if I'm standing here talking to man that looks like a wet dog. Why don't you step under here with me and stay dry?"

He did. With no traffic for the moment in either direction, two young sisters, no more than ten, ran giggling across Fifth Avenue. At the center, they stopped and pirouetted in place several times, turning their faces to the rain, before running to the opposite curb.

There were no marching suffragettes to be seen.

"How are things going with your Irish woman, if you don't mind my asking?"

"I'll admit the war has complicated things," Nolan said.

"So she's not coming?"

"She is. She plans to make the crossing out of Liverpool next month. But it's ... well, it depends on the war news."

"I read ships are being sunk all the time."

"Freighters and such, yes."

"Aren't the passenger ships in danger too?"

"The German submarines go after the cargo ships."

"But there's danger for the passenger ships, isn't there? I heard some carry supplies for the British."

"That's only a rumor. I believe the passenger ships are safe for the time being."

"Sounds very dangerous to me. But of course, it's your situation to think out, not mine."

They were silent for a moment. The rain grew heavy enough that the drops could be heard pelting their shared umbrella.

"Captain Gates said you have a fear of crowds," he said.

"Some days, yes. But not all days."

"Did something in particular happen to give you this fear?"

"Oh ... nothing in particular. I suppose it comes from everything that's happened."

"But nothing specific."

"Specific? Not really. Not that I can think of."

The cold rain grew heavier. For a moment, they both watched in silence as a nearly empty bus rolled by. Nolan became aware of something else. Her still presence so close to him. Just inches away. Her pale white cheek nearly touching his. Their hands, both holding the umbrella shaft.

The situation was made more difficult by the perfume and

the pink spring dress she was wearing, especially when all the women in sight were wearing somber, black winter coats.

Nolan realized that at no time in the last year had he stood this close to any woman, let alone one so attractive. He nearly groaned at the terrible burden of his own loneliness these many months, loneliness he had managed to banish from his thoughts for weeks at a time. However, at present, he could not.

"There's no possibility of a parade, and I'm getting cold," she said. "I'm going home. If you want to join me, I could make us some tea."

"I can't, but thank you. I have to keep looking for your sister. I'd be wasting time."

"Wasting?"

"Ma'am, it's your sister. You know what I mean."

She sighed. "Of course. You're right."

Then she turned and walked away on her own.

THAT NIGHT, HE searched through his steamer trunk and found his favorite photograph of Sheenagh, the one of her standing in her Sunday dress in front of the family cottage. Her playful but knowing smile brought her fully to mind.

He stared deliberately at the photo, as if taking medicine, waiting for thoughts of Julia to subside.

A second look at the evidence

24

The Threat

～✦～

NOLAN HAD LEARNED that confidence got you in a door in New York faster than anything else, so Monday morning he walked into the Second Branch Detective Bureau and then up the back stairs to the Evidence Repository as if he had official business there. He was not stopped.

The same clerk was behind the counter.

"I don't know if you remember, but I was the detective who looked at the Dutton evidence file a few weeks ago. I'm wondering if I could have another look."

He slid a Liberty head quarter across the counter and under a sheet of paper. Clyde winked at him and went to find the folder.

In the same empty interrogation room, still smelling of antiseptic, Nolan tipped over the folder to slide out the thick photographic sheets. Additions had been made to the file. Flannery's program from Proctor's Theatre and his ticket stub also fell out, as did Sarah's passport, containing more than two dozen stamps from countries she had visited.

Several new evidence photos had also been added. There were photos of the back alley and of the windows of the cook and the maid who claimed to have seen the robber. There was also a staged photo of the express package delivery agent standing on the front steps of Sarah's apartment building, pointing at the window through which he had observed that her apartment had been ransacked.

He went through all the photos and other items several times, trying to puzzle out a new theory. What could he see that he had not seen already? He was certain the truth was staring back at him.

He looked at the ransom note photo for an especially long time, feeling a rising frustration that no new clarity was emerging from any of the evidence.

After returning the file, he was on the way down the back stairwell when he met Cochran coming up. There was a startled look on Cochran's face when he recognized him.

"What're you doing here? Why the hell wasn't I told?"

"I didn't see you when I came in."

"And I'll bet you didn't come looking for me neither." Cochran suddenly rushed at Nolan, pushing him against the wall on the landing.

"I'm gonna say this only one more time, you little shit, and you damn well better listen!" He jammed his pudgy index finger into Nolan's stomach, repeating the action several times during the warning that followed. "I told you to give me any evidence you find and notes of people you talk to. I go to talk to the stepfather last week and what do I hear? You already did. Why don't I have notes of this on my desk, you stupid little shit?"

Nolan could have dropped Cochran even without the ring, he was sure. Although Cochran was larger, he had spent too many hours behind a desk and a lunch counter. However, Nolan knew he could not fight back, not against the police.

"I was going to give them to you," Nolan said.

"I want them yesterday, not tomorrow."

"I'll get them to you, I promise."

"You damn well better! My captain's pushing me hard on this case because someone up higher is pushing him hard. You understand?" With that, Cochran reared back and punched him in the stomach. He doubled over in pain, the wind knocked from him.

"And if I feel like it, I'll do a lot worse so's you won't be walking for a few months."

Cochran continued up the stairs, muttering under his breath. Nolan took a moment to recover his wind and his dignity before leaving the station.

TIERNEY WAS HANDING out bullets to four of his detectives, who were headed upstate to Poughkeepsie. They were going to guard a silk-dyeing plant where workers were out on strike. He was standing the bullets up in a line on his desk, six to a customer, as Nolan walked in.

Tierney looked up. "I got something for you." He paused to take an envelope out of a desk drawer. "A letter."

"For me?"

"Yeah. I knew what it was so I opened it. Figured you wouldn't mind."

He sailed it across the room, but Nolan also knew what it was before it landed on the floor. He could see the same messy block printing on the envelope's address.

Tierney handed the detectives train tickets as they pocketed their ration of bullets. "You know the rules. Only fire in self-defense."

"Such as if they throw rocks?"

"Depends on how many they throw."

"Such as if they swing clubs?"

"Depends on how many are swinging them."

The envelope, sent through the mail, had no return address. Nolan drew out the folded letter. The same smudged block printing, the same black dagger, skull, and hand at the bottom.

> To our friend John Nolan,
>
> You think you move so your safe? We can always find you!!! No one escape the BLACK HAND!! You DOG!! You DOG!! You DOG!!! Leave the Newark man alone or else a terrible end will come to you!!
>
> THE BLACK HAND

Nolan read and reread it, wondering what he should do now.

The detectives left, and Tierney sat at his desk, looking at Nolan who was still studying the letter. "When was the last one. A coupla weeks ago? That says it's an empty threat if nothin's happened in two weeks."

Nolan sat down in a chair, and as he did, he winced visibly from the lingering soreness left by Cochran's punch.

"Cousin, don't worry so much about this."

Nolan rubbed his stomach. "It's not the letter."

"What then?"

"I was at the station house, and Cochran cornered me in a

stairwell. He tells me I haven't been giving him everything I've been finding, so—"

"What you've been finding? It's none of his damn business."

"Well, he says it is and he threatened me."

"How?"

"He said I won't be walking for a few months if I don't give him everything I have."

"He said that? The bastard!" Tierney rose and walked to the window, repeating "bastard" as he stared out on the Hudson.

"He also caught me with a punch I didn't expect. The thing is, he's the police," Nolan said. "You can't fight the police. You can't even defend yourself. You know what they can do to you if they decide to."

Tierney was silent for a long moment, continuing to gaze out the window. "Cousin, don't worry about it."

"What is it I shouldn't worry about? The Black Hand blowing me up or Cochran crippling me?"

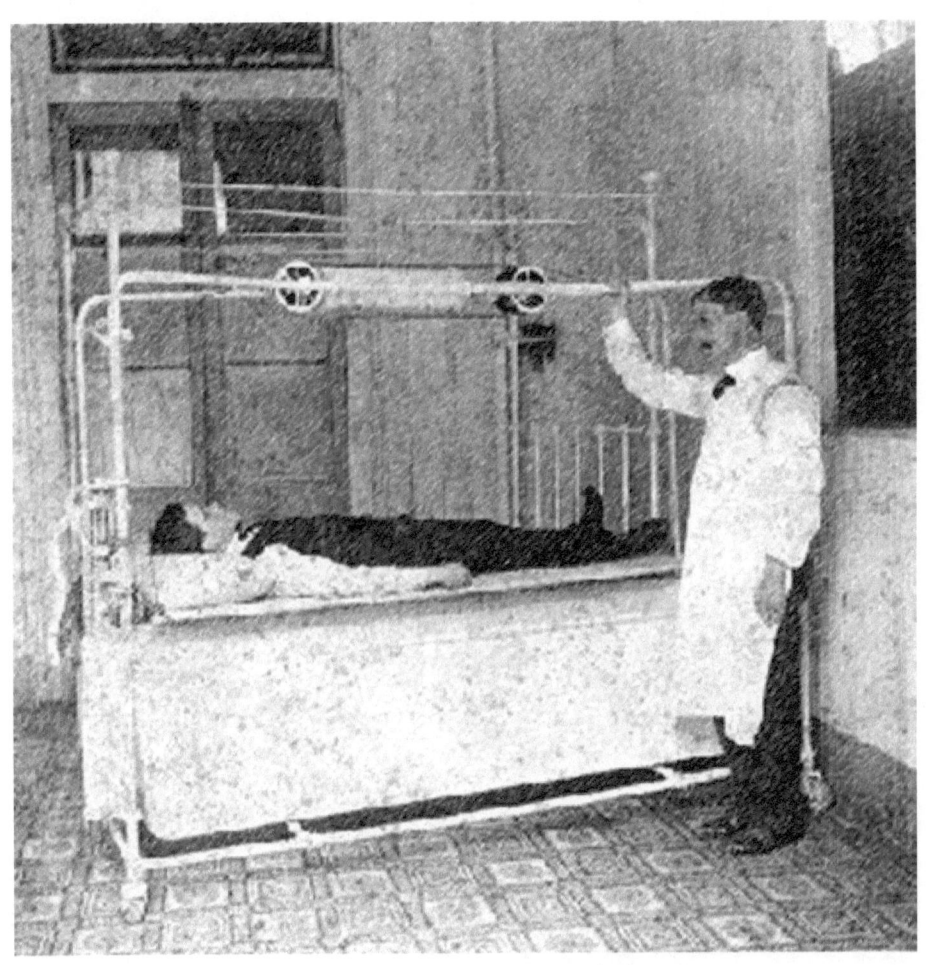

New York Hospital

25

A Hospital Visit

~✍~

Asales of Chaplin socks, hats, pins, squirt rings, and playing
cards in shops around the city.

One item, sold for a penny, was a Charlie Chaplin coin made
of lead, with a likeness of the actor on one side and a wreath and
stars on the other. It was discovered that the disk was the exact
size and weight of a nickel and could be put to use in vending
machines in the city's subway system to obtain chewing gum,
caramels, and other pleasures. Thousands showed up in the
collectors' boxes each day.

Tierney's agency was one of many contracted by the city to
track down the establishments still selling the Chaplin pieces,
deemed counterfeit coinage and thus illegal. Nolan had been
instructed to start his day by checking several shops near
Times Square.

As Nolan was heading out the door, the phone rang. It was
Gates. He had gotten another ransom letter, and this time it
was going to be hard to stall.

"He wants me to be at the train station in New Brunswick,
over in New Jersey, tomorrow at exactly five minutes to noon.
I'm to wait at the public phone there for him to call. He's
going to have instructions for me. I'm supposed to, uh … I'm
reading … 'Have the money in a sturdy valise, and have a ticket
to get on the twelve-ten train to Monmouth Junction, and sit
on the right side of the car by the window.' John, I'm afraid he's

thought of a way I can't get out of this any longer, so I've got to give him real money. I'm asking you and the police detectives to think this through and come up with a plan. I'm depending on you and Sarah is depending on you."

After hanging up, Nolan thought of two possibilities. The first was that the kidnapper would put a confederate on the train to pick up the valise. During the telephone call, he would tell Gates—and indirectly, the police—that if his man were stopped or arrested, Sarah would die.

There was a more likely possibility, however, based on the instruction to sit by the window and have the money in a sturdy valise. The kidnapper would have Gates throw the valise from the moving train to his motor waiting alongside the tracks. He had heard of blackmailers doing this before. The police would have no idea where the man's machine would be waiting. Gates would be given instructions by telephone just before the train left, leaving the police no time to get in position.

With all this on his mind, Nolan left for the trolley and to check for the Chaplin coins. At the third shop he went in, Russell's Dry Goods, he pushed through the crowd of customers to find a Chaplin coin in a sale bin. When asked how many others he had, the clerk smiled knowingly.

"Only what's there. Don't get caught. The transit police is keeping their eyes out."

Coming out of the shop, he was walking toward an idling streetcar when a small man, who had also been in the store, tapped him on the shoulder from behind.

"I heard you was looking for Chaplin slugs. I know a place sells them by the hundreds."

He motioned Nolan into a side alley, as if he needed privacy to tell his secret. Nolan went in only about twenty feet, but the man kept gesturing that he follow him farther. Nolan had a bad feeling and stopped. Then he glanced back and saw a much larger man had followed them in.

Now the smaller man ran by Nolan to join his partner in blocking his exit.

"Let's go, friend. Wallet, please."

Nolan reached in his pocket with his left hand and drew out his detective badge, flashing it quickly in hopes it would pass for a police shield.

"You're under arrest," he said. He drew his revolver even though he knew it was unloaded. The two bullets he had with him were in his pocket.

The smaller man instantly fled. The larger man, who had a drooping mustache and a hulking stature, turned as if about to run and then stopped. "A lot of boys I know carries their pistol unloaded," he said, "unless they think something's gonna happen."

Nolan calmly pocketed the badge. "It's loaded and once I pull it, I'm always willing to use it. No one'll fault me since I warned you."

"I'll bet it's not loaded, friend."

"Want me to prove it? Take a few steps my way."

The man thought a moment and then took one small, tentative step. Nolan continued to point the revolver at him. Emboldened, the man took another, putting Nolan to a decision. He could not hold his ground, but believing a fight was always the last resort, he chose to turn and sprint down the alley toward the service road behind the shops. As he ran, he holstered the revolver and moved both arms behind his back, where he transferred his ring to the appropriate hand. He could hear the large man behind him, but apparently unused to running, the thug labored in the effort, his heavy shoes pounding the paving stones.

At the alley's end, where the service lane began, Nolan darted around the corner of the building, put on the brakes hard, and tucked himself against the wall. Out of breath, fist clenched, ring ready, he listened for the approach of the plodding footsteps.

"YOU'RE ACTUALLY LUCKY you needed stitches. If you didn't, you would have gone home thinking this wound would heal itself. It wouldn't have," the doctor said as he pushed the needle and thread through the bloody gash on Nolan's thumb. He had already washed the wound with soap and water.

Nolan was sitting on a gurney behind a portable screen in the emergency room of New York Hospital. He had waited to see a doctor for more than an hour, his hand wrapped in a bloody newspaper. The people around him in the waiting area were moaning and crying, and the stench of blood, vomit, and unwashed bodies was overwhelming.

"It didn't look that bad," Nolan said, trying not to wince as the needle and thread were pulled through his flesh.

"It's not. It's the germs that get in there that are. You punch a man in the mouth—isn't that how you said it happened?—then you get all those germs in his spit into the gash and that leads to septic poisoning. Not a good thing. But I cleaned it and you'll be fine once the stitches come out."

Now a nurse leaned behind the screen. "Doctor, congratulations. I heard."

"Thanks," he said and she left. The needle entered again and the thread followed. "What happened to the fellow you hit?"

"He's either in this hospital already or in another one."

"Did you have him arrested?"

"No. I just left him there in the alley. I didn't want my name on some court paper so he can find me again. He's not going to be happy with what I did to his teeth and jaw."

The doctor smiled. "Understand." He peered closely at his finished work. "I can't tell you how many fingers and hands I've amputated of men who got in fights in saloons, punched someone in the teeth, and a week later they showed up here with a swollen and blackened appendage."

Another nurse leaned in. "Doctor. They told me what happened. Great work."

"Thanks very much," he said and she left. "What were you investigating that you got yourself into this kind of trouble?"

He told the doctor about the Chaplin coin and the vending machines. As he was relating the full story, he realized how trivial it must sound to a man with such life and death concerns.

"But I'm on a much bigger case right now," Nolan said. "This was one of the small things that comes up."

The same nurse returned, peeking behind the screen again. "By the way, were you the first to do that?"

"Don't know, but I do know I won't be the last."

She left again and Nolan had to ask. "The first to do what?"

"A man got caught in machinery in Hempstead out on Long Island over the weekend. He was bleeding to death, but there was no doctor around. I live on Staten Island, right near the aerodrome at Oakwood Heights. Someone got the idea to fly me up to the Hempstead Plains in a military biplane to suture the man's arteries. He managed to live. Quite an experience."

The doctor trimmed the excess thread from the stitches. "So, Detective, you said you're working on a big case. What is it?"

Nolan, still marveling at the idea of a flying doctor, felt not even the Dutton kidnapping could elevate him in this man's eyes. "Oh, a girl that got kidnapped just before Christmas in the city."

"Have I heard of the case?"

"The Dutton girl? The papers have been writing a lot about it."

"Why, sure. Quite a story."

Suddenly an idea struck Nolan. "Doctor, let me ask you. Can anyone hire one of those biplanes? Just an ordinary person?"

The Nieuport biplane with the pilot

26

The Pursuit

❧

THEY ASSEMBLED IN Gates' office in Times Square at seven o'clock on Tuesday morning, January nineteenth, one month to the day since Sarah's abduction. Nolan, Gates, Cochran, and two detectives assigned to Cochran by the police commissioner. It was still five hours before the ransom was to be delivered.

Nolan arrived early so he had a chance to read the latest ransom note. The childish scribble and Sarah's signature matched the first note, which remained in the hands of the police. However, the tone sounded different, as if written by someone smarter. Instead of "It will end bad for her," the note said, "It will be an unpleasant fate for your daughter."

Was the kidnapper now trying to appear more intelligent? Why would he bother?

Cochran acted as if he was in charge. He wanted to invite reporters, but Gates demanded it be kept out of the newspapers entirely. "If we miss him and he gets away with the money, then he reads about what we tried to do, he'll kill her for sure."

Cochran sneered at Gates when he turned away for a moment. The other detectives smiled. "All right, this is my plan," Cochran said. "We'll have men in disguise out at the New Brunswick Station, and we'll have other men boarding the train out of Newark. If we don't grab him at the station, we'll get him on the train."

"He won't be either place," Nolan said.

Cochran glared at him, the glare now a smirk. "Is that so, sonny. And where's he going to be?"

"The note is very specific. Sit by the window. Have the money in a sturdy valise. He'll have Captain Gates throw the valise out the window onto the tracks. He'll only tell the captain where to throw it during the phone call."

Cochran was silent. Evidently, he had not considered this possibility.

"Then we'll put men in cars along the tracks," he said.

"I talked to the station master in Jersey City. He said there's a lot of scrublands between New Brunswick and Monmouth Junction, and no roads in most of it. If your men walk into those scrublands along the tracks, this kidnapper will see them and never come out to pick up the money."

The room pondered his words in silence.

"Then what do we do now?" Gates asked.

"Well, I thought of something," Nolan said. "There's an aerodrome on Staten Island. I talked to a pilot, a man named Quenault. He's keeps a Nieuport two-seater there for racing in derbies. He's willing to take me up to follow this train, if Mr. Gates will meet his price.

"Why of course I will. Whatever it costs."

"We can do both, I guess," Cochran said. "Sounds daft to me, though, so I'll have men on the train and at the station anyway. We'll see what way it goes."

Nolan rolled out a map on Gates' desk. They all gathered around, Cochran reluctantly.

"In New Brunswick," Nolan said, pointing to the spot on the map, "there's a farmer who's an aeroplane enthusiast. He has a grass field pilots sometimes use to land, here, right near the Marconi Wireless Station in Somerville, just a few miles away."

By ten o'clock, Nolan would be there with the biplane, binoculars, and a map. If Gates got the call and it was instructions where to throw the valise, he was to immediately call the farmer. It would contain real bills this time.

"This is his number." Nolan handed the captain a slip of paper. "Once you tell us where on the tracks it's to be thrown, we can be over the station in five minutes."

"WHEN WE'RE UP, if you start to feel sick, lean forward and keep looking at your feet," said Quenault, a Louisiana man not much older. "The first time flying, it can be a shock."

The grass field was pocked and rutted, and as the biplane took off, Nolan, riding on a wooden seat, felt every bump in his rear end. However, once airborne, he was surprised at the smoothness. Nolan and the flyer, in the forward seat, were exposed to the wind in the open cockpit. Both wore goggles.

As the ground receded and he could see more and more of the countryside, it was not stomach sickness he felt, it was an exhilarating thrill that coursed through him. Did an accountant ever experience such a day as this? With most days rising above freezing now, any remnants of snow were disappearing from the landscape, leaving wet ground and leafless trees. Nevertheless, it was a beautiful sight.

The instructions to Gates, as Nolan anticipated, had been to throw the valise from the moving train. The kidnapper, using a different voice than in previous calls, spoke of a large, red, corrugated iron storage shed on the right side of the train, about 2.3 miles out of the New Brunswick depot. Gates was to try to hit the shed with the valise. "If the train stops, your daughter will be dead," he told him.

Nolan put the map in his lap, trying to locate what he was seeing below. Fortunately, the day was sunny. At a thousand feet, the binoculars were not yet necessary.

Suddenly the train tracks were visible and he shouted forward to Quenault. "There. The tracks. We follow them to the right."

The New Brunswick station was soon visible as well, with Gates' train already stopped and taking on passengers. As Quenault banked the plane to the right, Nolan hoisted the binoculars, focusing until he could clearly see ahead on the tracks. Yes, there were miles of scrublands to the side, with low bushes and small stands of stunted trees. And no, there were no roads to be seen in this desolate stretch.

Then he saw the red iron shed and leaned up close to Quenault. Nolan pointed. "There's our shed."

Quenault took the plane higher. The plan was to circle the area from an elevation of about two thousand feet, but do it inconspicuously, keeping in a wide circle above it.

Nolan checked the pocket watch Gates had lent him. Eleven minutes past noon. As the plane had risen, the temperature had dropped. On the ground, it had been nearly forty degrees, melting whatever snow remained, but Nolan guessed that at this height it was in the twenties. He pulled the wool scarf the pilot had given him tighter around his neck.

With the binoculars, he surveyed the acres of scrublands around the shed. Then he saw something unexpected. A motorcycle. It was standing between two bushes about a hundred yards from the shed and would not have been spotted easily from the ground.

Nolan scanned the rest of the field. At first, he almost missed the form huddled in bushes closer to the shed, but when it moved slightly, he knew this was his man.

Quenault maintained a slow, lazy circle over the area. With the binoculars, Nolan stayed focused on the figure in the bushes, but he tried to keep the railroad tracks in the periphery of his vision. Would the man look up? If he did, would he think anything of it? One saw machines in the sky all the time these days. However, the engine was quieter than Nolan thought it would be, even sitting ten feet away. He hoped this man would be so focused on watching the tracks and searching for any police prowling the field that it would not occur to him to glance upward.

Suddenly the New Brunswick train was chugging by on the tracks. Nolan's heart pounded. He did not see the valise come out the window, but when the train was past, he saw the man in the bushes dart out and run to the tracks. He picked up something lying on the gravel bed and ran back into the scrublands toward the motorcycle.

Quenault apparently saw the man too. He turned to Nolan, pointed, and silently mouthed the words, "Is that him?"

Nolan nodded.

They were on the scent. The man reached the motorcycle, climbed on, and soon was weaving north through the brush toward the edge of a sparse forest, which was as much open field as stands of trees. Quenault took the plane lower. It was easy to keep the binoculars on the motorcycle, Nolan found.

Within a half mile, the man turned onto a dirt road. Quenault stayed with him. The motorcycle was moving at a speed not much different than the biplane.

Nolan was able to follow the motorcycle onto a paved road and then, in several miles, into an area of small farms, vegetable fields, and pastures. When it turned into a driveway and disappeared into a wooden barn, Nolan, who had marked his map, tapped the pilot on the shoulder.

"All right. I've got him."

AFTER LANDING BACK on the Somerville farm, Nolan called the number Cochran had given him, a local police station in New Brunswick where Gates and all the detectives and agents had gathered after getting off the train in Monmouth Junction. They had a matching map so that Nolan could give them the location of the kidnapper.

Nolan learned of the outcome two hours later when Gates telephoned him in Somerville. In several machines, Gates' men had driven to the barn the motorcycle had entered and raided it in force, all carrying shotguns, none of which had to be fired. The man gave up with no fight and handed back the valise with all the money still in it. Martin R.J. Owens, according to his operator's license. He did not have blond hair, and Sarah was nowhere on the property. Owens said he had never met the girl.

Through techniques Nolan was never told about, ("I'll just say he needed a doctor after we were done," Gates said), Owens admitted that his brother was a clerk who worked weekends at the 42nd Street Precinct Station in Manhattan. The brother had gone into the evidence file and copied the handwriting and Sarah's signature.

"We have nothing," Gates told Nolan, his voice tired and frustrated. "We're back to where we were. I'll never see her again."

"Sir, I don't know if you saw the *Tribune* today."

"I did. You're about to tell me about the Italian importer, aren't you? His kidnapped boy."

"Yes, sir. His son was gone more than a month. Even though this importer didn't pay, the kidnappers let the boy go. Maybe Sarah's kidnappers have grown to like her. Maybe—"

"You know what kidnappers do to pretty girls? I'd almost rather they killed her, if they haven't already."

"But she might be alive, sir. You can't give up hope."

Gates sighed. "We'll see, John. We'll see."

Newsboys with an extra

27

War News

∽

THE NEWSBOYS WERE on every corner, waving extra editions in the air. Rushing to catch a trolley on his way in to the agency, Nolan heard the cry from one, "German submarines sink ships at Liverpool! Extra! Extra! Passengers in lifeboats!"

Immediately, his mind made the connection. Sheenagh. The passage from Liverpool. If the Germans were out to sink passenger ships now, Sheenagh could not risk making the passage. She would have to stay in Ireland. But the war might go on for years. The trench lines never moved, from what he knew. Shells and bullets flew back and forth with no advantage gained by either side.

He stopped and paid a penny for the *Morning Telegraph*. As he rode the streetcar, he read so intently that he missed his stop. After getting off at the next, he stood on the sidewalk until he finished.

According to the dispatches, a German submarine sank two ships close to the shipping lanes at Liverpool. In one incident, it sent a torpedo into a British coastal steamer, killing fourteen people. In the other, it sank a small, nearly empty liner on its way to the boatyards for painting.

His mind raced. What to do now? Should he go back to Ireland, put his own life at risk instead of hers? Or should they stay where they were and just endure the wait?

As he walked to the agency, he bought editions of other

papers, stopping periodically to read them. Approaching the building, he heard his name called.

"Mr. Nolan, might I talk to you a moment?"

It was Cochran, stepping out of a Dodge touring motor at the curb. Nolan backed away slightly as he neared.

"No, this is nothing bad, friend. I just want to talk. Why don't we go over here?"

Cochran led him to an alley, but Nolan would not enter. Cochran sensed the reason and stepped back onto the sidewalk.

"Look, friend, we just misunderstood each other is all. We can both do our jobs on this. I don't have to know what you're doing. We're both trying to do the same thing, which is to solve this case. Isn't that right?"

Nolan saw he expected an answer. "I guess so."

"It sure is. On the same side in this fight, really. We both want to save the girl. Let's shake hands and get on our way." Cochran extended his and Nolan tentatively took it. Cochran took a step toward his motor before turning. "You tell Sean we spoke. All right? Tell him everything is okay between us."

Completely confused now, Nolan nodded.

"And say hello to Sean for me too. Tell him we shook hands."

"I will."

"Remember. Tell Sean." He got back in the runabout and left.

Nolan watched the Dodge drive away, shaking his head. Tierney had something on him, for certain. His laughter died when he remembered the newspapers in his hand and his bigger problem.

Tierney was putting on his holster when Nolan entered the office.

"Got to go," Tierney said. "You're to call Gates, though. He needs you."

"Detective Cochran says hello."

"He talked to you, did he."

"He talked to me very nicely."

"Good for him. I got to go."

Tierney rushed to the door, but Nolan stepped in front of him. "Sean, thanks."

Tierney smiled. "No one puts a hand on my little cousin, Cousin."

Once he was out the door, Nolan called Gates' office and was immediately put through.

"I just got a call from Julia," Gates said. "She wants your services today. She's going somewhere and thinks she needs a bodyguard."

"Was she threatened?"

"No, she's just got a feeling."

"Sir, I was hoping to spend the day following Flannery."

"No, guard Julia. I don't give a damn about Flannery. Why's he even a suspect? He already had the jewels 'cuz he had my daughter. Why would he steal them from himself or kidnap her? If Julia feels she needs protection, then guard her. I couldn't live with myself if something actually did happen and I said no to a bodyguard .... Gotta go. I got another call, my girl tells me."

THE CADILLAC IMPERIAL limousine was carrying them to the Ritz Carlton for a society luncheon. It was a hired motor that came with a chauffeur in starched gray livery. They sat in the rear.

"Can you tell me what the nature of your feeling was?" Nolan asked her.

"I can't say it had a nature," Julia said. "It was just a general feeling that I should have a bodyguard, if I'm going to be going all over the city."

"But you said you're going to only one place."

"For right now, yes. But the day isn't done. By the way, did you hear about the ships being sunk in Liverpool? Didn't you say your friend intends to make the crossing from there?"

Nolan looked away. "Yes, I did."

"That must upset your plans for her. She hasn't come over already, has she?"

"No."

"Well, it looks like she's missed her chance, missed it entirely, if what I read is correct. Now she might have to stay in Ireland for the duration." She glanced over at Nolan, who kept staring straight ahead, not wanting to meet her eye.

"We'll see," he said.

"You'll see what?"

Now he looked directly at her. "I'll see if there isn't some way for us to be together because that's my intention—for us to be together."

The silence that followed seemed to embolden Julia, giving

her voice an edge. "A woman can't wait forever, Mr. Nolan. Girls like her want babies. That's their entire life, their babies. She might despair as the years go by. She might meet someone else in Ireland, marry him, have her babies; then where will you be, Mr. Nolan?"

He did not answer.

"You'll be right here in America," she said, "doing your detective work ... all alone."

"We'll see," he said. "The war might end tomorrow."

He knew that was not true, so she knew it too. He should have said nothing.

The limousine drew up to the Ritz Carlton and took its place in a line of motors delivering their passengers, nearly all well-dressed young women.

"What do you want me to do?" Nolan asked. "I take it I shouldn't go in to the luncheon with you."

"Sit in the lobby and wait. I'll be out in an hour or two."

"Or two?"

"Or three. Or four. You're getting paid, aren't you? Do what you're told, Mr. Nolan."

Preparing to write a letter

28

A letter to Sheenagh

❧

HIS ROOMMATE ASLEEP, the apartment quiet, he set a kerosene lantern on the kitchen table and found writing paper. First he reread Sheenagh's most recent letter.

January 7, 1915

My dearest John,

 This is just a short note today as Aileen & I are cooking & cleaning for the arrival of my parents here to Dublin. This may be the last time I see them as I'm resolved to make the passage to America before the German submarines make it impossible.

 I have not saved as much as I hoped these past weeks as I bought two new dresses & some cotton shirtwaists & shoes & two hats for America. Therefore I've decided to purchase a steerage ticket for the crossing. I know you advise me to come second class but it means a few days of deprivations in exchange for many many days looking like I belong in America.

 More & more I feel my soul leaving Ireland & tugging at me to go to America. It's like a child who has hold of your arm at the spring fair pulling you to move faster to see the next great thing up ahead. I read everything I can about America & life there. I yearn to be there with you. I take out the photograph of you & your sisters as often as possible to stare at you. A girl should not tell that to a boy. But there, I've said it. I won't say it again else it gives you a bad impression of me. But girls have thoughts that some think are only reserved for boys.

I miss you terribly & altho I have never set foot in America I already miss it terribly also.

Forever your Sheenagh

January 20, 1915

Dearest Sheenagh,

I can't say this strongly enough. Do not even entertain the thought that you'll purchase a steerage ticket to save money. You'll put your life in danger if you do. Buy a second class ticket. It will cost about 25 American dollars more but I have enough money now to more than make up for the difference. In my past letters I don't believe I spelled out for you how horrible and sickening a situation crossing in steerage was for me. So I want to do so now.

You have no assigned place to sleep. You're forced into the bottom of the ship with the chugging and clatter of the engines all around you into a room packed with beds and bunks from one side to the other. By the end of the first day the smells will be foul and the stinking will be inescapable. You have no privacy for your toilet and the crying babies and moaning people sickened by the rocking ship will fill your ears making sleep impossible. For a few precious moments a day you will be allowed out on the rear of a lower deck but instead of clean air you will be getting the dirty air from the ship's stacks and hold. Worst of all is the food. It is entirely inedible.

By the end of the ten days at sea—if you're not sickened or dead—you will land in Manhattan. The first and second class passengers will be examined by courteous doctors at sea just prior to arrival and then they will be allowed to step off the ship in dignity at the pier in Manhattan. But you'll be herded like cattle onto barges at the pier and transported over to Ellis Island. There you'll be dragged through lines of medical examiners and customs people probing you and asking questions for hours. If no sign of disease is found you'll finally be allowed to return to Manhattan by the ferry. Please, Sheenagh. I beg of you. Pay the money for second class. You'll be in a small cabin with only a few other women and will have your own toilet facilities. The food will be decent and you will have the chance to breathe clean wonderful sea air on the spacious upper decks. Please. Please. Please. I want a girl to arrive in New York City who I can marry and not a corpse who I'll have to bury.

You've likely heard the news of the Germans sinking two ships at Liverpool. I don't believe this changes anything for us. The latest news I've read is that they were mainly cargo ships and the few passengers on them were not the target.

By attacking these ships the Germans may have concocted a mistake they will grow to regret. They don't want to bring the Americans into the war and that's what many in this country will be calling for if liners carrying Americans become targets.

So please do not give up. Let's just watch the news for the next few weeks to see what happens.

I'm still working on the same kidnapping case but unfortunately I'm no closer to finding the man who did it. The stepfather was my main suspect but I find nothing he has done that leads to this. The brother is my best suspect at the moment but I have no evidence yet that he was involved either. It's very upsetting that after so many weeks I'm no closer than I was at the start and this girl is still missing. In fact as of yesterday she's been missing four weeks. Every other day I talk to the girl's father but he seems to have given up. He barely says anything during these calls now. I feel I've done my best and he has told me the same thing several times but it haunts me that I can't find her.

I'm close to finishing my business courses and my bank account is sufficient for both of us now even if you had not a single pound. Sean says he will give me a graduation gift of twenty dollars the day I get my diploma even though he knows I'll be leaving. Forget anything I've ever said unkind about him. I've come to like him.

So the only thing in our way now is the Germans and their intentions.

Please do not give up hope because I'm not. I feel our marriage is one of God's projects that he intends to see done right.

Forever your John

A Broadway streetcar

29

The Blond Man

❧

THE PARCEL POST clerk was checking a record book. The packages destined for Sarah's building in the weeks before Christmas would have been delivered from the 32nd Street office, the largest branch office in the city.

One of Nolan's theories was that perhaps Sarah received a package after three o'clock, establishing a different time for the kidnapping. After all, the evidence establishing the time—the two women looking onto the alley—was circumstantial.

"Her last name again?"

"Dutton. Sarah Dutton. And it would have been on the nineteenth, a Saturday."

"I've got the page but," he was slowly moving his finger down the sheet, "I'm not seeing anything. Four deliveries to that building out of this office, but for other people. Not for Dutton." The clerk closed the book. "Sorry."

Outside on the sidewalk, Nolan unbuttoned his greatcoat. The temperature seemed almost spring-like. He was reaching for his diary when he glanced over at a line of people waiting to board a streetcar on Broadway. It was as if lightning hit him. The blond man was one of the men on that line. He wore no hat in the warmer weather and his shaggy blond hair was unmistakable.

Nolan took note of the streetcar's destination from its front sign. The Battery. He rushed to his motor parked in the alley. Managing to start it on the first crank, he was soon out on the avenue, following the streetcar south. At each stop, he would pull to the curb and watch who got off. At the first stop, he loaded his revolver and transferred his ring.

At Prince Street, he saw the blond man through the streetcar's rear window. He stood and was beginning to file to the front. Hurriedly, Nolan parked in an alley and mixed into the thin crowd on the sidewalk, easily spotting the blond head a block in front of him.

Would the man lead him to Sarah?

At Spring Street, the blond man stopped to look in a tobacconist's window, so Nolan stopped and looked in a pharmacist's window. When Nolan glanced over, the man was running south on Broadway and was already near the end of the block. *Damn.* He had been spotted.

Nolan took off after him. He sprinted three more blocks down Broadway and then around a corner onto Canal Street, hardly gaining any ground and feeling his legs already tiring. At Varick Street, the blond man cut around another corner, but when Nolan took the same turn, he had vanished.

However, a street bay to a brick warehouse was open. Nolan could not see any other way the man could have disappeared. He took several deep breaths to regain his wits as he checked his revolver again. Then he cautiously entered the bay.

In a cotton and wool district, Nolan knew that rich smell, having raised sheep growing up. Bales of wool were stacked against every wall in the massive, two-story room. The dim light came from the open bay and from the filthy grated windows that ran along the ceiling. The floorboards were oiled wood, worn down and polished by years of horses and trucks moving over them. The walls were red brick, blackened by years of coal soot.

Nolan quickly moved into the shadows for protection. After a moment, and seeing and hearing nothing, he took a tentative step out onto the floor. A pistol shot rang out. Nolan slammed himself back into the bales, hearing the thud of a bullet into the wool two feet from him. His heart pounding, he pushed his body farther into a space between bales and kept still.

Where had the shot come from? He had no idea. The sound had echoed in the cavernous room, so he could not tell if his position was in or out of the direct line of fire.

His heart still pounding loud enough to hear, he waited and

listened. Was there another exit? Would the shooter have to run by him to get out the bay door? Did he have Sarah hidden somewhere in the warehouse? From the street, the building had appeared to be eight or more stories, which meant there were other storage rooms above.

Suddenly he heard distant footsteps, as if on wooden stairs. He stuck his head out and saw legs rapidly ascending a staircase at the far end of the room and going through a door to the next floor. Nolan ran across the wooden floor, toward the stairs, his revolver drawn.

As he reached the stairs, another pistol shot rang out from beyond the doorway. The bullet hit the staircase's wooden railing on the brick wall, inches from his hand, then ricocheted onto the floorboards behind him. Nolan dove to take cover amid the bales of wool at the base of the stairs.

The silence returned. What now? If he tried to climb the stairs and go through the door, he was a fat target.

He kept still and tried to think. Minutes ticked by. The blond man was as trapped as he was. There was a freight elevator at the other end of the room, but it would travel too slow for an escape route. This was a standoff.

His legs ached, as much from his curled-up position amid the bales as from the running. He was suddenly aware of how close he had come to death. Inches. At the time, the bullets hitting near him had been just a small part of the blur of events and excitement since spotting the man getting on the streetcar. Now they seemed to be the only events that had any meaning. Two bullets. Inches from killing him.

Then he thought of Sheenagh.

Catching this man and finding Sarah Dutton had taken over his life. It seemed to be nearly all he thought about. Now, crunched down in the bales of wool, the rich smell, evocative of Ireland, overtook him, and he felt a shift in his thinking. His goals were horribly wrong. Being alive to meet Sheenagh when she docked was and should be everything. A job was just a job. And he had no desire to be a detective a year from now.

If he had been considering a rush up the stairs, he now knew he would not risk it. He did not budge from his position. Keeping his revolver pointed at the doorway, he glanced toward the second staircase and resolved to stay put as long as it took.

Ten minutes later, a city patrolman stuck his head in the bay door.

"Anyone in here? I got a report of shots."

"Yes, over here! I'm a private detective."

Keeping an eye on the doorway, Nolan moved cautiously back across the wooden floor. Out on the sidewalk, he told the officer about the pistol shots from a suspected robber, and soon two more officers and several detectives arrived from the First Precinct Station.

They searched the warehouse for nearly an hour but found no trace of the man or Sarah. However, a window on the third floor was found open, and from there an iron fire escape led to the back alley.

Sing Sing Prison in Ossining

30

Sing Sing

~∿

CAPTAIN GATES HAD once raised funds for the state Democratic party alongside the man who was the warden at Sing Sing. Thanks to this connection, he was able to get Nolan an interview with a convict who worked in the prison paint shop with the Carnellis, the brothers of Dutton's mistress.

Nolan boarded the noon train on Friday out of Grand Central Terminal for Ossining, an hour upstate. The train was crowded with the families of convicts, many with children and most carrying food baskets.

The conductor announced that the smoker car was off-limits, since it was conveying the latest group of prisoners to Sing Sing. Hoping to see what a murderer, arsonist, or burglar looked like, children rushed forward to the car's door. Nolan thought it interesting. Were not their own fathers and brothers murderers, arsonists, and burglars?

At the Ossining Station, nearly the entire train emptied, and the crowds, three and four abreast, made the half-mile walk to the prison gates as a light snow fell. The new prisoners, in handcuffs and shackled together, trailed the procession. Children, with their parents' blessings, would rush back, gawk at the prisoners, and rush forward to their families.

Identifying himself at the gate, Nolan was taken by a guard to the cell block where he was to meet warden Osborne and the convict. They were waiting for him outside the man's cell, along with a guard. From there, they went to an assembly room in the same building. As they walked, introductions were made. Osborne never mentioned Captain Gates, which told Nolan he was not happy about the arm twisting that had led to this interruption in his routine.

In the large, empty room, Osborne told the convict, a small wiry man named Frank Cooke, to sit in a single chair that had been placed in the middle of the polished wooden floor. Everyone else surrounded him.

"We're going to make this quick," Osborne said. "Frank, this man wants some information I know you have. Just be forthright. And remember, this stays secret or else."

"What about what I asked in return for helping?" Cooke said.

"What you asked about what?" Osborne said.

"The band."

"You want to play in the prison band?"

"Yes. I play the piccolo. They don't have one."

"How do you know the band needs a piccolo player?"

"All bands do."

"We'll see," Osborne said. "And what about the Danish fellow I told you about, his offer? I'll let you go on this man's expedition if you give this detective his information. Wouldn't you like to go on a trip?"

"I don't know anything about Brazil, even where it is."

"It's in South America."

"All I know about South America is my brother said when it's summer here, it's winter there. You said this man wants convicts—"

"Convicts with good behavior."

"For a summer expedition into the jungle. So it would be winter there. I don't want to be out in a jungle in winter."

"The expedition would be in summer, so I take it he means you'd leave here in winter."

"That's just as bad. They have malaria in summer down there. I'd get malaria."

"Frank, for God's sake, just tell this detective what he wants to know."

"What about the band? The piccolo. You said this'd be worth something for me."

Osborne blew up, growling under his breath and walking away several steps. After taking a moment to compose himself, he returned, leaning in close to the convict and squeezing his shoulder. "Frank, let's start with you answering his damn questions, and then we'll see about the band."

Cooke sheepishly nodded his head.

Nolan was all business. Did the brothers have a friend with blond or light-brown hair who was paroled in the last year? ("Not that I ever seen.") Did the brothers ever talk about the kidnapping of a New York City girl named Dutton? ("Not that I ever heard.") What did they talk about? ("It was mostly in Italian, so I don't know.")

More questions brought no more information, except that one of the brothers played the tuba in the Sing Sing band. ("He's the one got me wanting to play piccolo for the Sousa marches.")

Nolan did not ask to speak to the Carnelli brothers, believing that if they were involved, they would only tip off their accomplices on the outside to his investigation. Once the interview was over, Nolan returned to the gate. Before leaving, he asked a guard if any blond convicts had been paroled in recent months.

"Only one I know of. A Swede, but he was nineteen and had a cancer. We sent him home to Minnesota to die, which he did, I heard."

On the train back to the city, Nolan struggled to think of what to write in his diary about the visit. He read through all his notes about the sister. Recently he had learned she had gotten work in a millinery shop on Third Avenue that had a sidewalk display in good weather. On a sunny afternoon several days earlier, he had stopped by to observe her while she chatted with browsers. He pulled his hat low, pushed his coat collar up, and stood nearby for fifteen minutes, as if part of the group waiting for a trolley. His notes were brief: "Kind and helpful."

Had she said anything, when he had gone to her apartment in the Tenderloin, that hinted she might be involved in the kidnapping? No. Had she said anything to hint she was even capable of being involved in a kidnapping? No. Other than admitting to the affair with Dutton, had she said anything to imply she was not a good girl trying to make her way in a world that was handing her nothing but poverty? No.

Yes, she had met Dutton at the hotel to talk after Nolan questioned her. So what? It did not prove a conspiracy to kidnapping, just a fear of being investigated.

Now, as the train rattled its way back to New York along the shores of the Hudson River, he stared out the window at the steep cliffs of the Palisades on the New Jersey shore. Living in the city, one could rarely see more than a few hundred feet in any direction. Gazing at the distant Palisades, he suddenly felt a wider perspective to his job and his life.

Eventually, he wrote in the diary: "I used to think only the best of people. Now somehow I have become a person who thinks only the worst."

Timothy Gates shows a painting

31

The Art Exhibition

✒

I T HAD TAKEN Nolan two days of telephone calls to get the man's name. Andries van der Linden.

Nolan learned from Captain Gates, who received a printed invitation, that Timothy Gates managed to have a painting accepted for a "new artists" exhibition that was running for two weeks at the Brooklyn Museum.

Nolan went to the opening, hoping to find young Gates there so he could confront him with the name. He discovered, though, that artists made a point of arriving late, if at all, to the first day's events.

"God forbid they give the impression they are anything but indifferent about their paintings being shown," an exhibition official, disheartened by the poor attendance, told him.

Late in the afternoon, Gates did turn up with several friends. Nolan waited until he could catch him alone. "Which is yours, if you don't mind my asking?"

"The geese. That one."

Nolan leaned in to study it. An oil, in extremely fine brush strokes, of three geese flying over the treetops. The painting was surprisingly good. "I like it. You have some talent."

"You like it because the geese look like geese."

"I admit that helps. I don't understand a lot of the newer—"

"My father thinks I'm stupid because what I paint looks too real. But that's what I'm trying to do, to make it look almost like a photograph. He thinks the artists that get paid the most these days never paint something that looks like it's supposed to look. He says I should be trying to make money, not art .... Is my father coming?"

"He can't be here today. He was busy. I think he planned on seeing it another time."

"So, why are you here? You like art?"

"I have a question." Nolan made sure he could see Gates' expression as he asked, "Do you happen to know where Andries van der Linden went after leaving the farm?"

"What's the name?"

"Andries van der Linden." Gates looked blank, as if he genuinely did not recognize the name. "He's the man you were friends with at the farm."

"You mean the man in the steam bath? That was his name?"

"Yes, two attendants recalled you talking together. He had blond hair."

Gates smiled. "I liked him. So Andries was his name. I thought maybe he was saying Andrew but because of the steam I'd heard it wrong. What'd you say his last name was?"

"Van der Linden. It's Dutch."

"Well, if you find him, tell him Timothy says hello, assuming he even remembers me. Tell him the fellow who liked his feet in a tub of cold water in the steam bath said hello."

Nolan studied his expression. There was nothing in it to say this was someone worried by the news that a detective had discovered his co-conspirator's name.

"I've been holding the wire for ten minutes already."

"It's Saturday and we're short some officers. I'm just filling in. Can you call back Monday?"

"It's important," Nolan said. "Andries van der Linden. Couldn't you ask some of the regular officers who are there?"

"You sure he lived here in Pottstown?"

"Yes, Pottstown. You're northwest of Philadelphia, isn't that right?"

He heard a heavy sigh on the other end and what sounded like the telephone earpiece dropping with a thud to the desk. In a few minutes, a different man, who identified himself as the shift lieutenant, came on the line.

"You're looking for Andries? Sure, we know him quite well here. Yes, the magistrate sent him to a treatment farm in New

York around Christmas. But he's back in jail here for being drunk and disorderly. I don't think he's the man you're looking for, though."

"What tells you that?"

"You told the other officer he ran from you and was quite a fighter?"

"Yes."

"He wrestled you to the ground?"

"I wrestled him to the ground, but yes, it was a real tussle. He escaped though."

"I don't think that's Andries."

"I'm pretty sure it is. Blond hair? Spent the winter at a treatment farm in upstate New York? He sounds like he could be the man I'm looking for."

"But Andries is sixty-two."

"Sixty-two?"

"Sixty-two. I got his arrest sheet right in front of me. In fact, I booked him. He's got bad rheumatism. And he might have once had blond hair, but it would be hard to tell now with so little of it left."

As he was about to leave Tierney's office for the day, Gates telephoned, clearly upset.

"The kidnapper just called me. He wants the ransom. I said I wouldn't pay unless I was convinced Sarah was still alive. He said he could see her plainly in the next room, that she was brushing her hair and reading a magazine. I demanded he put her on the telephone, John, and he wouldn't do it. He wouldn't do it! I said, you either put her on the phone or you don't get the money. John, he said nothing. He paused, then just hung up. She's dead. I'm sure of it. She wasn't in that room and she's dead and I'll never see my poor Sarah again."

After a moment's silence, Nolan attempted to say something, anything. "You can't be certain, Captain. We have to continue investigating as if she's still alive."

"But she's dead. I know it. You're right, John, you have to keep on, but I'm certain she's already gone." Then he hung up.

Julia and the letter

32

A New Ransom Note

Ｍonday morning, Tierney met Nolan on the sidewalk outside the agency.

"Gates called. His other daughter—"

"Julia."

"Yeah, Julia needs a guard outside her door for the morning. Gates will have someone to replace you by this afternoon. He says she got a letter of some kind."

"What's the letter say?"

"He said you're not to concern yourself with it. Just stay outside her door and leave her alone. Don't talk to her. He repeated that a coupla times. Leave her be. Just guard her."

Only after Nolan knocked loudly and repeatedly did the building manager come up out of the basement to the locked front door.

"I'm the detective here for Julia Gates."

"You mean Dutton."

"Sorry, Dutton."

He let Nolan in. "What's this about?"

"Oh, probably nothing. I'm just standing guard for the morning."

The manager retrieved the cane chair from the basement, and Nolan climbed the stairs with it to the second floor. Julia's apartment door was open slightly, and he could hear her sobbing inside.

In fact, he did not want to talk to her. He assumed she had

invented a drama to bring him there. He positioned the chair in the hallway and sat quietly. However, the crying continued and he began to wonder if maybe something he was there to prevent had happened.

Tentatively, he peeked in. She was visible through a side-room door, sitting on a sofa crying. A sheet of paper was in her hand, which he took to be the letter.

"Julia?"

She looked up with a start.

"Your door was open. Is everything all right?"

"No. What are you doing here?"

"Your father sent me. He wants me to stand guard. He told me about the letter."

Her sobbing grew worse. Nolan saw a stack of clean handkerchiefs on a side table and took several to her.

"Oh God. This is so embarrassing," she said. "Even if we pay this man, what's to say he won't keep the jewels and try to sell them anyway? He betrayed me once already."

Nolan realized she believed he knew what was in the letter. He kept quiet and sat in an armchair.

"And this threat about going to the police. It's blackmail," she said, still clutching the letter and its envelope. "He'll get nothing from that. My father will deny it. I'll deny it. He won't be able to prove it."

Nolan nodded agreement. "He won't get away with it."

"Just because he was my chauffeur doesn't mean anything."

"Do you mean the chauffeur at Christmas? Who drove you up to White Plains? I thought you said he was South American."

"I had to make you think that at the time. But even if you knew it was him, it wouldn't have helped you. He still got away with the jewels, and I didn't know his full name or where he lived. Oh God!" She broke into tears again. Between heaving sobs, she vaguely pointed to the apartment door. "Please close it. Someone'll hear."

Nolan went out to the front room, his mind flying through the implications. Her chauffeur had robbed and kidnapped her sister, and somehow Julia had found out it was him. Why would she want to keep that from him or the police?

It also meant the chauffeur was the blond man, the man who had tried to kill him, the man he was searching for.

Nolan returned and sat again. "Julia, your chauffeur has

blond hair, isn't that right?" She nodded. "I thought you said he was with you in White Plains the whole time you were there."

Sniffling and wiping her nose, she looked up and stared at him silently, puzzling something out. "What did my father tell you, exactly?"

"That you got a letter. Can I see it?"

"That's all he told you? He didn't tell you what it said?"

"Not entirely. Can I read it?" He held out his hand, but she folded it up and stuffed it back into the envelope. Then she rose and went into the bedroom, shutting the door.

Nolan stood outside. "Julia, it would help me if you could tell me everything that's in it. There may be clues to finding him and stopping this."

"No," she said.

"Can you at least tell me this much …. When you were up in White Plains, did he leave you after dropping you off and then go back to the city to rob your sister?"

She did not immediately answer, but after a bit, she came out again, more collected and holding only the handkerchiefs. "He must have. He must have driven back to New York to rob her." She sat on the sofa and dissolved into tears once again. "Please leave. I don't want to talk about it anymore."

"But if you—"

She rose now, her face flushed with anger. "No, no more! Get out! Get … out!"

Nolan knew to leave. Once in the hallway, he heard the apartment door lock, and then he heard Julia talking quietly on the telephone, the conversation punctuated by long silences on her end.

Sifting through the possibilities, Nolan came up with a theory. As Dutton had suggested, Captain Gates had somehow colluded with the chauffeur to steal back his daughter's jewels. The chauffeur took Julia to White Plains, then he drove back to New York, but the robbery went wrong. Sarah came home early, so the chauffeur—the blond man—took the jewels and her. Now, in addition to the ransom demands, he was blackmailing Gates through this letter to Julia, threatening to tell police of Gates' role in the crime.

Around noon, with Nolan sitting in the hallway, there was a knock on the main door downstairs. He went to the railing and saw the manager answer it. He heard his name mentioned and then saw one of Tierney's burly detectives at the bottom of the stairs.

"Captain Gates wants me to relieve you. He says go back on the case this afternoon. Which door is the girl's?"

Nolan pointed and they passed on the stairs.

"One more thing," said the detective. "Gates says—and I don't know what it means—he says to keep everything you learned to yourself until he can talk to you, but 'find the son of a bitch'—his words, not mine."

Above the grocery, a man in the window

33

The Suspect Found

∿

PEOPLE WERE CREATURES of habit, Nolan believed. If the blond man picked up a trolley at Broadway and 32nd, he would likely do it again. So he parked his motor near the southbound trolley stop just after lunch. Before beginning the watch, he went to a pay telephone in a hotel near Greeley Square and called Gates' office.

"I heard Julia told you some of what this is about," Gates said.

"She did. Some of it."

"Well, this man wants more money."

"Julia used the word 'blackmail.' "

"What's the difference. Ransom, blackmail. He wants money."

"Sir, blackmail about what?"

"It's no one's business. He wants money is what he wants. Look, I need you to find him, find his location, but I don't want you to confront him. I know you think you can take him, but don't attempt it. Call me first. I want to be there and I'll bring more men. Do you understand?"

"Yes, sir."

"I mean it. Don't engage the man. Just find out where he is, no matter how long it takes, and call me."

Gates said he was unsure of the name of the chauffeur who worked for Julia only a few times, but he was searching household billings to find it.

Nolan kept watch all that afternoon and evening, then began again the next morning. During the night, winter had overtaken the city again without mercy, and the temperature had not risen above twenty through the morning. As he sat in the Ford, he rocked back and forth to keep warm, his gloved hands rubbing his ears to stop them from going numb.

Finally, at nearly dusk he spotted his quarry. The man walked within three feet of the open window of Nolan's machine. Even though he was wearing a hat, Nolan recognized him. The blond man took his place in a crowd waiting for the streetcar, which Nolan could see approaching behind him, four or five blocks up Broadway.

As he waited for the trolley to reach them, Nolan put on a straw boater and eyeglass rims with the lenses removed to make himself less recognizable. Despite Gates' instructions, he also loaded his revolver and moved his ring to his left hand. He would not be unprepared.

Once the trolley was at the stop, he pulled his motor in behind it. Fortunately, like a creature of habit, the blond man sat by the rear window of the car where Nolan could easily see him.

A dozen blocks down Broadway, the man stood to get off. Nolan, his heart racing, saw no parking spot, so he followed in the motor at a slow speed as the man walked south, staying a block behind.

When the blond man stopped to look in a store window, Nolan had no choice but to drive past him to the end of the block on Broadway and then pull to the curb and wait for him to pass. When the man did not go by, Nolan glanced back. He had crossed Broadway and was about to go east on 17th Street. Nolan lost sight of him. He jumped out of the motor in pursuit, afraid that he would be too late to see what building the man entered.

Once he was on 17th, his eyes darted up and down the street, but the man had vanished. Except for a few people outside a grocery, examining produce, he saw no one. He had lost him.

Nolan stood in the shadows of a tenement doorway opposite the grocery, watching for any movement in doors, in windows, on roofs, angry that he had taken his eyes off the man. The sun gone, there was little illumination on the street other than lamplight from tenement windows.

Ten minutes went by. Nolan was ready to give up when a window shade lifted on the floor above the grocery. The blond man, without his hat, sat right by the window and read a newspaper. A miracle.

Was Sarah sitting in the same room, tied up and gagged in a chair? Furious, Nolan wanted to charge up the stairs and break down the door, but he knew he could not.

Deep enough in the shadows to be sure he was not visible, he wrote the address in his diary and then went back to Broadway in search of a public telephone. He found one several blocks away in a hotel near Union Square.

Gates was not in his office. However, he once gave Nolan the telephone number of his residence by Central Park with the warning never to call it unless there was a dire emergency.

Nolan located the number in his diary. Gates answered immediately.

"I've found him, sir."

"Honestly?"

"He's got rooms on 17th Street, right at Broadway. I watched him from the street. He's there now."

Gates wrote down the address.

"Leave him be," Gates said. "Just wait out on the street where you can't be seen."

"There's a doorway across from the grocery on the corner. You'll see me."

"Then wait there. I'll arrive in thirty minutes. John, I knew you were the man for this."

Nolan went back to the tenement doorway. He picked up a single sheet of the *Evening World* that had been blowing down Broadway and pretended to read as he waited, burying his face behind the paper with only the occasional glance at the window.

When he saw the captain's red Pierce-Arrow coming down Broadway, he rushed to meet it. Gates, his driver, and three other men Nolan had never seen—huge men with the mean look of strike-breakers—got out.

"Point me to the window," Gates said.

They walked to the corner and Nolan pointed. "What's the plan now, sir?"

"The plan is for you to go home. You've had a long day. Leave it to us from here on." He clamped a fatherly hand on Nolan's shoulder. "John, you've done your job well. I knew I was right when I hired you. Your final check will be more than usual, quite a bit more. Thank you."

"Don't you want to call the police first?"

Gates looked back at the window, taking a deep breath. "I don't want to call them yet. I want to do this my way, not theirs."

At that point, it was clear Gates expected Nolan to leave. Reluctantly, he did. Once in his auto, he backed it up to a point where he could see the grocery building through the rear window. He watched as Gates and his men crossed the street and went in the front door.

If Sarah was in there, whether dead or alive, they were going to kill him, Nolan was sure. That had to be the plan all along. Gates wanted this man to suffer the way his daughter had suffered, the way he had suffered. If Gates was behind the robbery in the first place, if he hired the blond man, he never intended her to be kidnapped or harmed in any way. That had been all the blond man's doing. And by killing the man, Gates would also extinguish any possibility that his own involvement would become known.

Nolan was glad he had been ordered to leave and not take part in it. Most likely that was Gates' intention—to relieve him of responsibility.

Nolan imagined their slow, silent walk up the stairs, everyone treading lightly, their pistols and revolvers drawn. Then what? The men would break down the door? A fight or gun battle would follow? Sarah would be rescued?

He watched and listened, his eyes and ears straining. It would be justice if they did kill him, he decided. What happened inside that apartment would be as God intended.

However, over the next fifteen minutes, only a brighter light going on in the room changed the situation.

At one point, Nolan got out of his motor and went back to the darkened tenement doorway across the street for a closer look. He still saw and heard nothing to indicate what was going on. No one came to the window, or even passed by it. He heard no raised voices, no gunfire, no sound of any kind.

Finally, exhausted, confused, and freezing, he drove home.

Western Union cablegram form

34

Foolish Thieves

❧

A HABERDASHER'S SHOP ON Fifth Avenue had been robbed three times in a month by the same thieves. In the middle of the night, they would take out the fanlight ventilator above the street display window, reach in with a pole hook, and quickly strip the showcase of ties, gloves, and silk hosiery.

Tierney's agency had been hired to guard the business from midnight to dawn, and with the Gates case apparently ended, Nolan drew the assignment. This was his second night sitting in the Ford in a dark alley opposite the shop but in view of it.

Along with a canister of hot coffee and a ham sandwich on the front seat, he had several newspapers. In the two days since Gates went to the blond man's rooms, Nolan had been expecting to read news of Sarah's rescue, the discovery of her dead body, or news of the blond man's arrest—or the discovery of his dead body. However, there had been nothing in the papers about the case. Mainly, they were filled with news of the European war.

Twice, Nolan had left messages with Gates' secretary asking for him to call. "Just say John Nolan would like to know how the situation at 17th Street ended." He received no call back.

He had decided that if Sarah had been found alive, he would have heard about it by now. So he believed she was likely dead, and now, certainly, the blond man was dead. Gates had exacted his vengeance.

Also on the seat next to him was the latest letter from Sheenagh. She had decided the crossing would be on the

Royal English Line's SS *Peterborough*, leaving from Liverpool on February first, four days from now. And she had agreed to come second class. The ship was set to arrive in New York on February eleventh, and its first-class cabins were likely to be carrying prominent Americans, lessening the chances the Germans would try to sink it.

The Irish papers had made the same observation as those in New York. The seas might be safe for liners for the next month at least, especially for those with American passengers, because Germany did not want to provoke America to enter the war.

Nolan wanted to send her a cablegram after his shift ended with more instructions based on his own experience crossing. Using the stub of a candle affixed to the top of the coffee canister with its own melted wax, he began to write the message on the Western Union form:

ALWAYS WEAR LIFE VEST—DURING DAY SIT NEAR LIFE BOATS ON DECK—BRING DRY CRACKERS FOR SEA SICKNESS

In his two nights guarding the shop, he had become acquainted with the night foot patrolman on Fifth. The man came down the alley now and idly leaned in the passenger window.

"Mr. Nolan."

"Mr. Foye."

"Anything from our boys?"

"Nothing yet, but it's early." Nolan extinguished the candle. "Look, can I ask you something. A man I worked for recently had me track down a fellow."

"Let me guess," Foye said. "His wife's lover."

"Good guess but no. So I found the man and gave my employer his address, but I never heard what happened. Let's say the man who hired me killed this other man. I'm not saying he did, but let's just say. Where do I go to find the names of people recently killed in the city?"

"You're assuming your employer left him in a state to be identified. I know I wouldn't've. But even if he didn't mutilate the face, the chances anyone in any morgue in this city would be able to identify any unknown body ... well, the chance of that is next to nothing."

"That's their job, though. To identify people."

"Let me tell you a story. Big Tim Sullivan, the crooked Tammany Hall boss .... You gonna eat all that sandwich?"

"Go ahead. Help yourself to half."

"You're a friend for life," Foye said, reaching in. "So Big Tim ... he died a couple of years ago. He was just fifty-one but he had syphilis and was suffering religious mania. Sometimes he still had some of his wits, though, so his brother up in the Bronx, where Big Tim also lived, hired a couple of men as nurses but also to play cards with him. Big Tim loved cards. So they were playing pinochle one night when Big Tim got up to piss but wandered off."

Movement across the street made them both turn to look. They stared silently for a moment.

"I can't believe it," Foye said. "Not the haberdasher's. The shop two doors up."

"I see 'em."

Foye stood erect and squinted across the avenue, brightly lit with electric street lights. "The fools. They haven't even bothered to look over here."

Two men, one carrying a ladder, the other a bag, had stopped and were unfolding the ladder in front of Weber & Lewis, the clothiers.

"Let's give them a few minutes to get set up and get into the crime," Foye said, leaning on the motor and taking another bite of the sandwich. Nolan quietly opened his door and stood, waiting.

"So ... Big Tim." Foye brought his voice down to a near whisper. "That night a freight train in the Bronx hits a man, and his body is taken to the Fordham Morgue. Everyone in the city knows what Big Tim looked like. Everyone. Even though the face on this body was untouched, even though this man was wearing gold cufflinks and a tailored suit, not a soul in this morgue recognized it was him. They classified him as a tramp, and he was set to go to a pauper's grave in the potter's field."

With both Foye and Nolan watching in astonishment, one of the men drew a telescopic pole from out of his pant leg, stretched it out, and attached a hook to one end with adhesive tape. The other, up on the ladder, had a screwdriver and was removing the ventilator cover's screws.

Foye shook his head in disbelief. "Idiots. Anyway, Big Tim. He got moved to two more morgues where no one recognized him, and he ended up at the Bellevue Morgue two weeks later. A friend of mine, another bluecoat, goes by Bellevue to see if anyone from our precinct is lying there. He sees Big Tim, immediately knows it's him, and says so. 'Look, it's Big Tim.' Everyone crowds around—the coroner, other doctors. 'You're right. It's Big Tim.' "

"What you're saying is don't count on the morgues to figure out the man's name."

"That's right. If you know what he looks like, go look at the bodies yourself, if you want to find him. Tell them your brother is missing, and you want to see if he turned up."

Foye took the last bite of the sandwich, drew his revolver, and unlatched the safety. Nolan reached back in the motor for his own revolver and moved his ring to his left hand.

Foye looked over at Nolan and whispered, "If you find him, though, and you know his name, you've got a duty to report it and what you know."

"But I'd be forced to give away the name of the man who employed me."

"Well, after all, he is a murderer."

Nolan was silent.

"Could you do me a favor?" Foye said, looking across the street again. "I'll walk up Fifth on this side and you walk down it. They don't look armed, so when I charge across the street at them, they'll run south. You go across also and see what obstacle you can present to that, Mr. Nolan."

The flower market

35

Buying Flowers

❧

A T DAWN ON a raw, cold Saturday morning, Nolan arrived at the flower market in Union Square as the vendors were unloading trucks brimming with hothouse flowers, including roses. Business had been good for the Saturday market, even in the winter. The vendors' purses would swell as the morning progressed, so the Union Square Commercial Association had hired him to walk guard on the crowded sidewalk.

Mainly, the customers were smiling, well-dressed men and women, sorting through the fragrant, colorful bouquets and bunches. Any light-fingered pickpockets or raggedy boys looking to lift a purse would be conspicuous, making Nolan's job easier.

The crowds before eight o'clock were sparse, so Nolan was able to think as he patrolled the sidewalk. He had a lot to think about. Sheenagh was preparing to make the crossing. Also, he had passed his last accounting exam two nights earlier and been interviewed for a job with an investment firm on Broad Street immediately after the exam results were posted.

He had still heard nothing from Gates about his daughter. It was the last week of January and nearly six weeks had passed since her kidnapping. Was there even a shred of hope left?

Late in the morning, as Nolan was absorbed in these matters, he saw a couple at a bucket of long-stemmed American beauty roses. The man, in a suit, had well-combed blond hair, but his face was turned away. Curious about the blond hair but expecting nothing, Nolan moved on the sidewalk to get a better viewing angle. He was shocked. It was *his* blond man, his arm entwined with that of a young woman who was pulling individual roses from the bucket as she made her choice. She had pretty though bland features and a flirtatious attitude. Nolan could not help but wonder if the man genuinely cared for her or if he planned to rob her too.

He moved closer, to within twenty feet, and stared at the man, unconcerned that he might be seen. What would be the consequence? He wanted this man to know that an adversary he had once tried to murder was standing close by and glaring at him. Absorbed in small talk with the woman, the blond man purchased several roses without ever looking his way. Then he and the woman crossed Park Avenue toward 17th, never looking back.

Nolan was stunned. How could he still be walking the streets of New York? How was his dead body not rotting in the garbage pits somewhere by the waterfront? At the very least, how was this man not in jail?

His shift did not end until noon, so Nolan prowled the sidewalk, pacing with agitation, as he mulled over his history with the man. He resolved to finally confront him face to face.

When noon arrived, he walked with purpose toward 17th Street. He navigated through the crowd of people buying fruits and vegetables outside the grocery, and as he reached the tenement's front door, a woman with an empty shopping bag emerged, greeting him as if he were a tenant. He tipped his derby and tried to enter before the door could lock behind her, but it was too late. About to turn away, he thought to try the door anyway and found it unlocked.

As he climbed the stairs, he checked his revolver in its holster. He found the correct door, stopped in front of it, and took a breath. The door of the next apartment was open and an elderly man in an undershirt appeared.

"Are you John?" he asked.

Startled, Nolan answered "Yes" without thinking.

"Well, the man what lives there, he tells me if John Johansen comes by, tell him he'll be back about eight o'clock tonight. He went to Staten Island on the ferry, a little sightseeing with a lady."

Nolan thought quickly. "You said John? I thought at first

you said Jim, which is my name. I came by 'cuz I heard from a friend this man might want a job. But I'll come back later in the week. No need to tell him anything. I'll just come back."

The elderly man nodded and closed his door.

The blond man

36

The Truth

❧

THAT EVENING, AN hour after sunset, Nolan parked his motor up 17th Street so that he could see the front door by the grocery.

The blond man returned without his woman friend about seven thirty. Waiting until the light in the second-floor apartment came on, Nolan got out and crossed the street, checking his revolver.

Inside, he climbed the stairs, which creaked loudly with his first few steps. He slowed his ascent, trying to put less weight on his shoes and more on the railing as he gripped it.

Once on the second-floor landing, he crept to the man's door and held his breath to listen. He heard steps across the wooden floor inside, but moving away. On a hunch, he gripped the door knob and ever so slowly turned it. The door was not locked.

He made a final check of his revolver and shoved open the door.

"Don't you damn well move!"

The blond man, still in his suit and bow tie, froze where he stood in the middle of the floor, holding a cup of coffee.

"Sit down! On that chair. Now!"

The man sat and Nolan, hearing some noise in the hallway as other tenants reacted to the shouting, closed the door behind him.

"Is anyone else here? Tell me now, damn it!"

The coffee cup trembling slightly in his hand, the man

shook his head. Nolan leveled his revolver squarely at him. He walked around the front room, opening doors to other rooms, looking for ... he knew not what. Sarah? That made no sense. However, no one was in the bedroom, the kitchen, or the front room closet.

"Where is she?"

"Where's who?"

"Sarah Gates. What happened to her?"

The blond man, whose breathing was coming fast, looked confused. "I have no idea."

On a side table in the parlor, Nolan found mail. "So this is your name? Andor Gulbrandsen?"

The man nodded sheepishly.

"What's that? Swedish?"

"Norwegian."

Nolan turned back to him and moved closer, the revolver pointed right at his face. "I know about your ransom letters. Why don't you tell me your side of this kidnapping, if you have a side. I don't think you do."

"I swear I wasn't involved in no kidnapping."

"So you say."

"If you know anything, you know I wasn't the one who planned this. It was only a robbery when it started."

"So you say." Nolan suspected he was talking about Captain Gates. "Let's hear it then."

The blond man shifted nervously in his chair. "Julia .... You know who I'm talking about, don't you? Julia?"

"Of course I do. Julia Gates, I mean Dutton."

"I was her chauffeur," he said. "It was Julia who wanted me to break in and take the jewels. She said it would be no problem and it wasn't."

The astonishing story he told over the next ten minutes seemed, to Nolan's mind, plausible. Fearing her sister wanted to marry a man only interested in her money, Julia schemed to "borrow"—as the blond man termed it—the jewels until after the wedding in order to take the money out of Colin Flannery's personal equation. Would he still marry Sarah if she had lost her fortune?

They had stopped at Sarah's apartment about two thirty that Saturday on their way to White Plains, knowing Sarah was at a charity event. Even though Julia had a key, the chauffeur broke open the rear door with the sledgehammer to make it appear like an ordinary robbery. He took the jewels from the trunk as well as a few other items, again to make it look like a random theft, then he left without ever encountering Sarah.

"We're sitting at the corner of Sixth in Julia's motor, the Dodge, getting ready to pull away, when the both of us—Julia and me—we both clearly see Sarah go in the front door. No doubt about it. When we left, Sarah was alive."

"Then what?"

"We drove to White Plains and I put the jewels in the spare tire. We didn't hear nothing about any kidnapping until her father, Captain Gates, called on Sunday in the afternoon. That's the truth."

"That's your version of it."

"It *is* the truth. Ask Julia. She saw her sister alive before we left. It wasn't us. I'd driven those two sisters to Sherry's, the restaurant on—"

"I know where it is."

"I'd driven them a few days before, and I'd driven for Sarah by herself several times. The coat Sarah was wearing that day, black with a gray fox collar—the coat on the woman Julia and I saw walk in that front door—there's not many like it."

"But you kept the jewels. You stole them from Sarah, then from Julia."

"Yes, I did, but that's been settled. Mr. Gates has them now. He knows the truth. Julia told him finally. He knows everything."

The blond man squirmed in the chair, his eyes riveted on Nolan and his revolver.

Nolan had to think a few moments. "So, who kidnapped her?"

"What do I think? You care what I think? You're pointing that revolver at me, ready to fire, and you want to hear what I think?"

"Yeah, I want to hear what you think."

"All right." He took a deep breath. "There's boys, rat boys, that goes up and down those alleys behind the rich apartments looking for valuables in the trash. I know because I was one of them when I was growing up. You find whole turkey drumsticks, a little nibbled off. You find uneaten apples and oranges. And once I found a perfect chocolate cake in its box from the Waldorf Astoria, only a coupla slices gone. My guess is one of these boys saw that broke open door and goes in. Then he's about to collect his rewards, but he hears the key in the front door and gets panicky. When Sarah came in, he decides to kidnap her. Just more money for him."

"He stole her car? This boy?"

"Some of 'em can drive. They go up to the Catskills in winter and steal motors out of the garages of those rich houses which is closed for the winter. I know 'cuz I done that a few times. But that's just my guess. I don't know anything more about it."

Nolan had to think. "Why did the maids who worked on that alley see you going in but never anyone else after that?"

"Were they still looking?"

"What do you mean?"

"People don't look somewhere forever. Maybe they walked away from those windows after they saw me."

Nolan and the blond man stared at each other until the silence became significant to both of them. Nolan had doubts now, and the blond man knew it.

Could this kidnapping have taken place the way the blond man said? And if Julia did plan the robbery, Nolan knew Gates could not have this man arrested, whatever he believed, without implicating Julia. That was why he was still free to walk the streets.

So that was what the blackmail letter to Julia had been about—her part in this and his demands.

Nolan took a seat on the sofa, still pointing the revolver at the man, trying to think. They stared at each other during a prolonged silence. After all the blond man had put him through, Nolan took pleasure in seeing stark fear in his eyes.

"Were you the one sending me the Black Hand letters?" Nolan asked.

As if ashamed, the man nodded. He drew out a handkerchief and wiped the sweat off his upper lip and brow, his eyes staying on Nolan's gun.

Shaking his head, Nolan rose and walked to the front door as he put the revolver back in his holster.

"Are you and me finished?" the blond man asked. "Is our business done?"

Nolan paused at the door, his hand on the doorknob. He thought about being shot at in the warehouse, the bullets hitting right beside him. He could still recall the sickening thud as one hit the bale of wool inches away.

He was about to transfer his ring to his left hand but hesitated. He looked back at the blond man.

No, he told himself. He was better than that and had better things to do with his life than risk going to jail. The ring stayed where it was. "Yes, I guess we're done."

As he rode the trolley home, he tried to make sense of what had happened. He was sure Gates believed one of two things. The first was that perhaps, just as the blond man claimed, he had no involvement in the kidnapping, and the identity of the abductor and the fate of Sarah were unknown. The second was that after he broke in and stole the jewels and left with Julia for White Plains, his confederate slipped inside the unlocked back door and waited for Sarah to return so that they might kidnap and ransom her. Nolan had no idea which was true, and at this point, it did not really matter.

Whatever the truth, Gates would not go to the police because Julia would be arrested as the instigator of the plot to steal the jewels. And apparently, being unsure of the truth, Gates was unwilling to kill the blond man himself.

In the end, Nolan felt he had to determine for himself what justice was and act accordingly, and he decided it was best served by leaving well enough alone.

In any case, he would no longer be part of the justice system by the end of the week. Hopefully, he would be an accountant. A *married* accountant. And justice would have to be reached in the world without any help from him.

The Parcel Post service counter

37
Judgment Day

❧

Thɛ Royal English Line office was near Battery Park on the southern tip of Manhattan. Nolan had gone to the office the past six afternoons asking for word of the *Peterborough*, and for the past four days there had been no reports.

"We seem to have lost contact with her," the desk clerk told him the first day. "But that's not unusual. Weather can take down the Marconi wireless."

Nolan knew a German submarine could also be the cause.

The last report the office had from the *Peterborough* came when it was still within the "zone of exclusion," the edge of which was one hundred miles west of the Irish coast. It was agreed upon by the warring parties that ships would be unharmed if they traveled beyond the line to the west.

When the locks came off the front door Thursday morning— the day the *Peterborough* was scheduled to arrive—the same man was at the desk. Seeing Nolan, he knew the question before it was asked.

"Still no word. But I wouldn't worry too much. The weather on the Atlantic has been rough this week and the wireless is touchy. We'll get a batch of reports from other steamers just before four o'clock this afternoon. Telephone me then. Maybe one will have sighted her."

The clerk gave him a slip of paper with the office's exchange number. His stomach churning, Nolan went outside, walked down to Battery Park, and sat on a bench to watch the tugs and ferries, the sloops and yachts, the freighters and steamships ply the harbor, as he tried to find his composure.

The day before, a letter arrived in the mail from Captain Gates containing two fifty-dollar gold certificates and a note thanking him for his "excellent efforts on behalf of my family." The letter contained no information about Sarah or the blond man.

The day before, Nolan had been offered employment in the accounting department of a Broad Street firm. He notified his cousin he would be quitting.

Nolan felt his true life, the idyllic life he long believed was patiently waiting in his future, was finally about to arrive. However, Sheenagh had to arrive first.

AFTER LUNCH OF a hot dog, too anxious to sit still, Nolan walked around the seaport until he found a Parcel Post office. He had bought a souvenir plate, requested by his mother, with depictions of Manhattan scenes—City Hall, a Broadway marquee, the Woolworth Building—that he wanted to send her.

"She and my father live in an apartment in Ireland, and they both work," he told the postal clerk. "If they're not home when your man comes, how will she get it?"

"A neighbor can sign for it. That happens all the time. If it's a private home, we can leave it on the doorstep or behind a bush, but we won't leave it in an apartment building unless it's signed for."

Nolan paid the charge and left, but as he rode the trolley up Broadway on the way home, something occurred to him. He got off at 32nd Street and went to the post office there.

He realized he still had his badge in his coat pocket. For what could be the last time, he flashed it to the service counter clerk at the Parcel Post window, who was sitting on a high stool, reading the *New York Times* during an idle moment.

"Excuse me," Nolan said. "I came in and spoke to you about a month ago."

"The kidnapping of that girl."

"Yes. You found there were several deliveries to her building that day, December nineteenth."

"But none to her, as I recall."

"That's right. But could you check to see if she signed for any of those other deliveries?"

The clerk, a man near retirement with a perpetual squint, sighed heavily at the envisioned work. "I'd have to go find the book again. That'll take some time, and there's no one else here to work the counter, as you can see."

"As you can see, there's no one on line either, other than me. Please, if you could."

The clerk sighed again, so Nolan took out some coins and slipped two dimes under the man's rate book.

"All right, let me see if I can locate it," he said.

As it turned out, the book was on a shelf right behind him so he only had to revolve on his stool to find it. He flipped through pages slowly and studied one for several seconds.

"Well, that's interesting. It turns out she did sign for one. It was a package delivered to a Mrs. Richard Holloway on the third floor. A Miss Sarah Dutton signed for it at the door. She probably kept it for her, if the woman was gone on vacation."

"Most of the tenants were gone," Nolan said. "What time was that?"

"Twenty-three past ten o'clock."

"In the morning or evening?"

"In the morning. Ten twenty-three a.m."

Disappointed, Nolan began to walk away, but the clerk called out to him. "Sir, wait. There's a note. The first attempted delivery was in the morning, at ten twenty-three, but there was no answer. The second delivery, when your woman signed for it, was in the afternoon."

"What time in the afternoon?"

"Looks like ...." He squinted more than normal. "Looks like five something. It's scribbled. Either five fifteen or five sixteen p.m."

"Can I see it?"

The clerk turned the book and pointed to the line on the page. No doubt. It was definitely a five. Five fifteen p.m.

And the signature. It was definitely Sarah's.

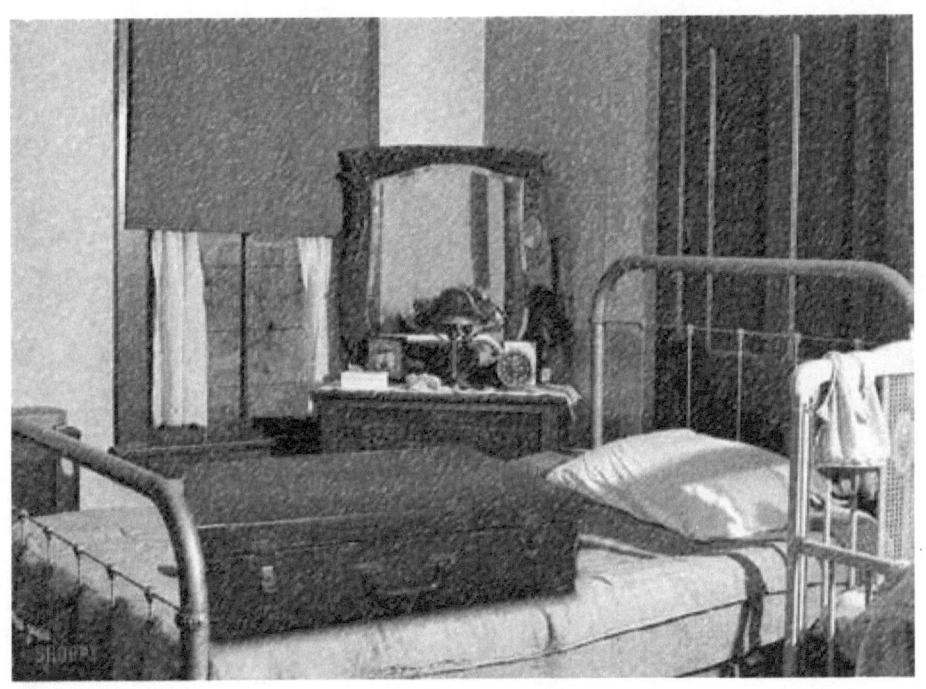

Packing to leave

38

Loose Ends

∾⌣∾

A FIRE DEPARTMENT MOTOR engine blocked much of West 44th Street in the Tenderloin. The pavement was still covered with puddles of water from a pair of early-morning blazes. A patrolman was not going to let Nolan pass a wooden barrier, thrown up to stop the public, until he showed his badge.

"They've already brought in you people, have they. Who hired you, the hotel?"

Nolan nodded sheepishly and was allowed past. He walked by the Hotel Gerard, where a blackened streak ran up the front of the building and wisps of smoke still rose from windows on the first floor. However, he was going to a boarding house across the street, a brownstone with a Greek restaurant on the first floor. Inside, a resident directed him to Colin Flannery's room on the third floor.

The door was wide open, and Flannery was evidently packing. A half-filled suitcase lay on the bed, although Flannery was not visible from the hallway.

Nolan knocked on the door frame. "Colin?"

"What?" The voice came from a closet.

"It's John Nolan. The detective. We've spoken a couple of times."

Flannery appeared and put a comb, brush, and shaving kit in the suitcase. "What's this about? I'm busy."

"Nothing to worry about. This is my last day on the case, and I've got to hand in the final report to Captain Gates. I just need to ask you a couple of questions, to tie up some loose ends. What happened to the hotel across the street?"

Flannery eyed Nolan suspiciously. "Just some dumb fire, someone cooking in their room, probably. But then a fire engine coming up Broadway turned the corner and hit the side of Vitagraph Theatre while trying to avoid a woman in the crossing. That started a second fire."

"A lot of excitement, I guess."

"Unless you was trying to sleep, or unless you was in one of those two buildings. Then it was just a headache."

"Well, the reason I .... Do you mind if I sit?"

"If you want."

Nolan sat on the only chair in the room. "Where're you going?"

"Boston. A friend lined me up a job. I need to earn some money. So I've got a train out of Grand Central in a couple of hours."

"Well, the reason I came by is to finish up a report on everything."

Flannery wadded up a shirt and mashed it into the beaten-up suitcase. "You catch that kidnapper yet?"

"Unfortunately, no."

"My guess is Sarah is dead and he's long gone, maybe to South America, with the jewels." Flannery went back to the closet. Nolan saw a pistol lying on the bed behind the suitcase. Nolan, who had come right from the post office, did not have his revolver with him.

"By the way, this is my last week as a detective. I'm quitting."

"Couldn't manage to find the kidnapper?"

"That's not the reason. I'm getting married and need better work than this."

Flannery, returning with a pair of trousers and suspenders, offered no congratulations. "So, what is it you want to ask me?"

"Let's see." Nolan studied his diary as if it held the question. "The nineteenth. As you know, the kidnapping took place around three. And I know you were at your job until six. I talked to several of the men you worked with and saw your time slip and signature. So, that all checked out and it goes into the report."

"Of course I was at work. The police knew that."

"As I said, this is just to tie up the loose ends. The other thing is the ticket to Proctor's Theatre for vaudeville."

"I gave the ticket stub and my program to the police. You want to see them, go talk to the police."

At the knock on the door frame, both Nolan and Flannery turned to where a man in a suit and fire department cap stood.

"You both live here?"

"He does. I don't," Nolan said.

"I'm a fire marshal. I want to ask what you saw."

"Nothing," Flannery said. "I was trying to sleep."

"You didn't get up, with all the sirens?"

"No. I didn't smell no smoke, no one was running around on my floor, so I guessed the fire was elsewhere."

"You didn't feel any responsibility to look out and investigate what was going on? Maybe go out and help some people?"

"That's your job, not mine."

The fire marshal glared at Flannery. "Well, did you see the motor engine that crashed? Did you see it come around the corner?"

"I didn't see anything, let alone stick my head out the window to see any engine crashing. This stuff happens all the time around here, fires and motor crashes. You get used to it. It's the Tenderloin."

"Well, sir, I hope if it's your building what goes up in flames, your neighbors are as helpful to the situation as you."

They were all silent.

"Is that all?" Flannery asked. "Anything else?"

Shaking his head, the fire marshal left. Flannery turned to Nolan. "What about you? Anything else?"

"One more thing," Nolan said, looking again at his diary. "The ticket to Proctor's. It didn't have the date on it. Unfortunately, the ticket man tore the date off before handing the stub back to you. It had the week, but the exact night of that particular show was torn off. Fortunately, the ticket said 'weekend evening rate,' so it had to be either the Friday, Saturday, or Sunday show."

His suspicions growing, Flannery stopped packing and sat on the edge of the bed.

"But this is probably nothing to worry about," Nolan said. "As it happened, Constance Evans was the headliner that entire week, but she got sick for the Saturday night show and the Beaumont Sisters filled in. That was the only night she was sick, so if that's the show you saw, the one with the Beaumont Sisters, that puts you at Proctor's that evening."

"That's the one I saw."

Nolan wrote something in his diary, and Flannery watched him.

"I recall thinking I could see Constance Evans another night," Flannery said.

"The Beaumont Sisters—how were they? I've never seen them," Nolan said.

Flannery seemed to relax now, almost breaking into a smile.

"You haven't seen them? They're actually quite good. They play a lot around New York. I've seen them several times at Fairchild's over on Seventh. Their act is a memory thing. The sisters are twins. One goes into the audience and asks twenty or so people to write down a big number on a paper. The person says their number out loud and is holding the paper so only the audience can see it. All the others are holding theirs too. Then the sister on stage, without being able to see these papers, recites them all back, right to left, so fast you have to marvel at it. I couldn't figure out how she did it."

"Maybe she just has a good memory."

"No one's got a memory *that* good. But you should see them. They're quite impressive." Flannery rose and continued packing.

"Did you finally get a chance to see Constance Evans? That was her only week in New York."

"No. She wasn't on that night, so of course I missed her. Maybe she'll travel to Boston. They have almost as many theaters as New York, I've heard."

Nolan put away his diary and rose. "I guess that's all that relates to you, Colin. Good luck in Boston. This has been an awful thing. I know it's upset your life terribly."

"It changed everything."

"You must have been sick when you found out about the robbery and the kidnapping. I know you thought Sarah shouldn't have kept those jewels in the apartment."

"I told her so many times to move them to a bank. If this hadn't happened, how different my life would be. What that money could have done for us."

"Again, I'm sorry for what you've gone through."

"Not as much as me, that's for sure."

"Where are you going to be working in Boston?"

"My friend is setting up the job. I don't know yet. The train is at three, so I have to rush and do some things. What's your new job, by the way?"

"Accountant."

He laughed. "That'll be different. So detective work wasn't your line, I guess."

"I guess not. Good luck to you."

Beneath Grand Central Terminal

39

Trapped

〰️

NOLAN BROKE INTO a run when he was a block away from the 42nd Street Police Station. In the Detective Bureau, he went right to the captain's office and knocked several times on the door glass until the captain, standing at a filing cabinet, turned.

"What do you want?" he shouted irritably.

Nolan, out of breath, opened the door slightly. "Sir, the Dutton case, the kidnapping of the Dutton girl. I'm a private detective."

Reluctantly, the captain waved him in. "I know the case you're talking about."

"The man who probably did it is about to leave town."

Now Cochran came to the door behind them. Nolan gestured toward him. "Detective Cochran and I have been working on this together, and I have some new information. But we've got to hurry."

He told them about Sarah's signature for the Parcel Post package late in the afternoon and about Flannery's ticket.

"The date on the ticket wasn't torn off. I made that up. And Constance Evans went on that night. I lied to him about her also and he took the bait. If he'd been there, he would have seen her. And the Beaumont Sisters. He took that bait too. They weren't on the bill at Proctor's that night. He was never there."

He told them about Colin's temper, his frequent arguments

with Sarah, and his anger about her keeping the jewels in the apartment.

"I'm sure he went to see her that night when she didn't show up at Proctor's, and he was already angry. She must have told him about the robbery and his temper exploded. Maybe he figured with all her money gone, what use was she to him now? So he cooked up this kidnap scheme. What happened after that, I don't know. Maybe Flannery got a friend to actually grab her and keep her somewhere, so she wouldn't know he was the one behind it. But as I say, I don't know. What I do know is this. He's lying about Proctor's, and you don't lie without a reason."

The captain looked at Cochran. "Detective?"

"It all adds up, it looks like to me. Maybe he's our man."

The captain gritted his teeth and slapped his thigh hard. "Well, finally. Let's go get this bastard!"

THE EXPRESS TRAIN to Boston was scheduled to leave Grand Central Terminal, just a block from the bureau, at a quarter past three. The captain, eight detectives, and Nolan gathered outside the Park Avenue entrance to the station and laid out a plan.

Only Nolan and Cochran had ever seen Flannery.

"Red hair, clean-shaven, six feet tall, has a crooked nose that looks like it was broke at least once," Cochran told them.

The captain decided that Cochran and three detectives would start at the front of the train and move toward the back. Nolan, who had borrowed a revolver from the captain, and three detectives would begin at the rear and move forward. One detective would remain at the platform entrance to make sure Flannery did not try to escape past them.

"Inconspicuous, fellows. Inconspicuous. Don't let passengers know you're police unless you have to, and no guns unless you have to. I'll wait out here and get you a patrol wagon. Good luck."

Just two years old, the terminal served mainly commuter trains and those to nearby cities. It was the largest and busiest in the world. Inside the main concourse, which had a high, vaulted ceiling depicting the starry winter skies, Cochran found a station agent with knowledge of the express. The train was made up of day coaches with a dining car, sleeper, and smoker thrown on—perhaps a dozen cars total. Track Twenty-Six on the upper level.

Nolan checked his watch. Departure was in eleven minutes. Flannery had to have found his seat by now. He thought of the pistol lying by his suitcase. Had Flannery packed it away or was he carrying it?

Once on the platform, Nolan watched Cochran lead his team to the front of the train at the far end, walking within a few feet of the passenger windows. At one point, he took out his revolver to check his ammunition so that anyone inside could see him. Nolan could only shake his head.

With his three detectives trailing him, Nolan entered the rear car, a day coach, with his hand on the revolver in his coat pocket. The car was half full, with several people in the aisles settling luggage on the overhead racks.

With one rapid sweep, Nolan's eyes took in the entire car. Flannery was not in it. The crew navigated the blocked aisle, Nolan focusing on the glass door ahead. Could Flannery be smoking in the enclosed vestibule between cars? Would he see them coming? His hand tightened on his revolver.

No one was in the vestibule. As they entered the second coach, a conductor stopped them and asked brusquely to see their tickets. A detective produced his badge and scowled, quickly shoving the startled man out of the way.

Again, Flannery was nowhere to be seen, and the crew moved rapidly to the next car, this one a sleeper. The train's engine suddenly fired up as it prepared for departure.

"The suspect doesn't have any money," Nolan whispered to his detectives. "He won't take a sleeper. It's too expensive. Let's keep going."

"No. The captain'll want us to check all the compartments, to give the car a thorough search," a detective said.

"But it'll waste time."

The detective was already knocking on the compartment door. "New York City Police! You're going to have to open up."

Nolan could not believe it. If Flannery was in there, a bullet might be coming through the door at any moment.

Exasperated, Nolan kept going toward the next car.

"Hey!" a detective shouted after him.

He did not respond or look back.

The next was another day coach. He was halfway up the

aisle, trying to see the face of a man in a hat who was standing with his back to him, when he heard the muffled crack of a gunshot in a car up ahead. Two more shots quickly followed. The glass door of the vestibule flew open and three passengers ran up the aisle toward him.

"Get down! A crazy man with a gun. He's shooting at people."

More shots rang out. Passengers began screaming. Mothers grabbed their children; husbands grabbed their wives. Some dove under their seats, others fled toward the back of the train in the rapidly filling aisle as panic spread. Nolan fought his way through them, pulling out his own revolver and holding it over his head.

"I'm a detective. Out of the way, please!"

Reaching the vestibule and letting several frightened people rush by him, he saw Flannery in the middle of the aisle of the next car, reloading. Then the far vestibule door opened and Cochran stuck his head out and fired at Flannery. The bullet missed but hit the glass of Nolan's door, cracking it in spider-web circles.

Flannery fired back at Cochran, who ducked into the vestibule. Then, almost as if he sensed Nolan's presence, Flannery turned and saw him. With a vicious look on his face, he fired. Nolan jumped to the side as soon as he saw the pistol being raised. This time, the glass of his door shattered and fell in pieces to the vestibule floor. Nolan waited a few seconds and peeked through the opening. Flannery was awkwardly climbing out one of the coach's windows and tumbling down onto the tracks.

Nolan opened his vestibule's door to the tracks and looked out to see Flannery running up the tunnel toward the distant light and freedom. Nolan jumped down, immediately worrying about the electrified third rail as he hit the gravel between the rails. How could he tell which one it was? *Just stay on the gravel and wooden ties*, he told himself.

Up ahead, Cochran and two detectives also dropped down onto the tracks. Then all were running, but Cochran, out of breath, was quickly left behind. One detective fired at Flannery but missed. In fifty yards, Nolan caught up with the two detectives. They were both young, one considerably taller than the other.

"What's his name again?" The tall detective yelled back as they all ran.

"Colin Flannery!" Nolan shouted, his voice echoing in the tunnel.

"Flannery!" The tall detective yelled ahead, firing again. "You hear me? We've got police at the end of this tunnel. You can't get out. Give up now!"

Where the track joined with others and the tunnel widened into a much larger tunnel, a cavernous room, Flannery suddenly darted to the side and into the shadows. Reaching the same place, Nolan and the detectives took shelter behind iron pillars.

"He can't go anywhere," the shorter detective whispered.

"He can go back on another track, then on to the station," Nolan said.

"I'd see him move," the shorter detective said. "I'm pretty sure I know where he is. You see that electric box, the big one by the wall? About thirty yards up? He's behind it."

"You got better eyes than me."

The shorter detective aimed and fired at the metal box. The bullet ricocheted off the cement wall just behind it, producing a puff of dust.

"Flannery, you see what I just did? I know where you are. Give up, now!"

"No." Flannery's voice was weak and plaintive.

"Maybe we got him with a shot," the tall detective whispered.

"He wounded one of us back on the train, so I hope he sits there and bleeds to death," the shorter detective said.

Suddenly the shorter detective rushed to a closer pillar, and seeing this, Flannery partially rose and fired at him. Nolan and the taller detective leaned out from behind their pillars and fired also. Then they were all shooting, revolvers punching out from behind metal barriers, the sharp cracks echoing throughout the vast tunnel, the smoke from four guns clouding the air.

With the shooting still going on, Flannery jerked to one side as if he had been punched. He stood for a split second and then fell forward on the tracks, face down. The detectives held their fire. When it was clear he had stopped moving, all three rushed him. The shorter detective removed the pistol from his grip.

Cochran, huffing and gasping, reached them now and stared at the body on the tracks. "Well, I guess I should go report this to the captain."

"Get an ambulance, too," Nolan said. "And you should tell the station master to hold all trains and to get a flagman out here to stop anything coming in on these tracks."

Cochran rushed off and Nolan crouched down. "Colin, can you hear me?"

Flannery groaned and slowly rolled over onto his side. A blood stain spread in the middle of his shirt, just above the belt.

"Got him in the stomach," the tall detective whispered. "Look at all that blood."

"Colin, why'd you shoot? They just wanted to question you," Nolan said.

"I didn't do nothing. You got the wrong man."

"No, we didn't," Nolan said with compassion in his voice. "I figured it out, Colin. Constance Evans wasn't sick that night at Proctor's. I made that up. She went on, which means you were never there. I'm afraid I caught you in a lie."

Flannery slowly opened his eyes, resigned to his fate. After a long pause, gazing only at Nolan, he whispered, "It was stupid."

Nolan softly squeezed Flannery's arm. "Tell me what happened. Where's Sarah?"

Flannery broke into quiet sobs, which caused him more pain. "I'm so sorry," he groaned.

"Colin, tell me where Sarah is. Is she still alive?"

"This is what happened." His raspy breathing was weak. "I went to her apartment that night and she told me about the jewels. But it wasn't me that decided to do this kidnapping. It was her. She knew her father would never give her any more money."

"Where is she now?"

Flannery put up his hand. "I'm going to tell you. We made her parlor look like she had to be dragged off. Then we drove her motor to the West Side, to the waterfront, and I paid a drunk to rent us a room in a rooming house. We spent the night there and wrote the first ransom note."

"Colin, please, before you faint, where is Sarah? Is she alive?"

He weakly held up his hand again.

"I was supposed to go to my job each day then come back to the room at night. She figured it would only be a couple of days before her father paid up." He paused to swallow. "But her photograph had been in the papers a lot, and she was afraid the landlady or a cleaning woman or someone would come in and recognize her. She didn't want to be sitting there reading a magazine and looking like she was part of the kidnapping. Then we'd both get arrested. So she had me tie her up and gag her."

"Is that where she is, still in that room?"

Flannery clutched his stomach, his pain evident. "I came back after work the first day and she was dead. I put on the gag too tight and she suffocated. God, oh God!" He was crying now. "I drove her body up to the river and put her in the weeds a hundred yards from where I left her motor car. You'll find her. She's wrapped in a blanket. For those other ransom notes, I copied her signature. It was all stupid, stupid, stupid." His weeping turned to sobs. "When I realized I'd killed her, I knew I'd killed myself too. I might as well've died right there."

"Just don't move. We called an ambulance."

Nolan took off his own coat and balled it up into a pillow for Flannery's head, which had been lying on the gravel between the track ties. A pool of blood was forming beneath him on the tracks.

Nolan stood. He and the two detectives still held their revolvers.

"Looks like only one bullet hit him," the short detective whispered.

"But in the stomach. That's not good. If you hit the liver or puncture the stomach—"

"We were all firing. Wonder whose bullet it was."

They looked at each other's revolvers.

"We all got thirty-twos."

"That means we'll never know for sure."

There was silence. Flannery had stopped moving. He was hardly breathing.

"It's better you don't know for sure whether you was the one killed a man," the tall detective said.

Nolan watched Flannery's face. There was a moment when the color seemed to drain from it suddenly, turning the skin a waxy yellow.

Later, he would wonder if that was the moment he died.

Nolan tells Gates what happened

40

The Sad News

∾∾

IN A COLD drizzle, he walked the six blocks from Grand Central Terminal to Times Square and Gates' office, trying to compose the unthinkable news he would have to deliver.

"Sir, I'm sorry to have to tell you this, but a few moments ago ...."

"Sir, this is going to be difficult for you, but this afternoon ...."

He imagined the poor man's face. He knew Gates had lost nearly all hope his daughter would be found alive, but Nolan also knew hope never left the soul entirely unless crushed by fact.

With that, he thought of Sheenagh and his own hopes. He winced with pain at the image that haunted his thoughts. Bodies and debris scattered about the gray, frigid Atlantic.

Up ahead, the huge electric clock in Times Square was visible as he approached on 42nd Street. Five minutes to four o'clock. He reached for the slip of paper in his pocket with the number of the Royal English Line office but knew his first responsibility was to talk to Gates.

Getting out of the elevator on the fourth floor, he took a deep breath. Approaching the open door of Gates' office, he could hear his voice. His secretary, in the outer office, waved Nolan through. Gates was sitting behind his desk, on the telephone. He briefly acknowledged Nolan with a wave of his hand.

"You say he confessed? Who heard the confession?" Solemnly, Gates glanced at Nolan. "What were his exact words?" Gates' face turned pale and his mouth trembled slightly. "And he was definite that she was dead? There was no uncertainty?" He turned away from Nolan toward his window onto the square. "Thank you for calling, Commissioner …. No, just tell me when you find her body. Again, thank you."

He hung up and stared out the window, his back still to Nolan as he sat in the desk chair. Then his shoulders started to heave in silent convulsions.

Stay or leave? Nolan had no sense of the right thing to do, so he stayed.

In a minute, Gates took a deep breath and leaned his chair over to a side cabinet. He slowly took out a small glass and an amber decanter. Turning, he lifted the glass as if to offer one to Nolan, who declined. He poured a glass for himself.

"You know, John," he drew out a handkerchief from a back pocket and blew his nose, "there are some moments you never forget. I'm sure you have yours. But, this moment I'm having, what makes it different," he searched for the words to express it properly, "is that it is one of life's final moments, one of the moments life hands you near the end of your days to make you think. I'm one of the wealthiest men in the city. Yet, my daughter lies dead in the weeds up in Harlem. My wife, my ex-wife, went into a sanitarium last week out on Long Island for a nervous disease. My one remaining daughter won't even talk to me. And my son, my only son, is a damned cocaine addict again and will have to go to the treatment farm upstate."

He slowly rose and stood at his desk, his eyes red and glistening. "Don't you see, John? Life adds it up for you so plainly that you can't miss what it's trying to tell you. You have all the money anyone could ever want, but you have nothing else. Nothing. Life wants you to understand. What does the money really matter? Does it matter at all, if you have so little else?"

Then his mouth suddenly trembled violently and he turned back to the window to hide his tears. "What does it really matter?" he whispered several times.

Nolan waited for nearly a half minute in silence until the silence, other than Gates' quiet sobs, became awkward. He knew it was time to leave.

"Sir, I just wanted to tell you how sorry I am. I … well, I'm so sorry ...." He let his words trail off rather than say more. Then he quietly backed out of the office.

HE FOUND A public telephone in the Knickerbocker Hotel on the square. He had to wait for nearly ten minutes behind a fancy-goods salesman making a pitch to a potential customer, growing more anxious by the second. It was a quarter past four. What if the shipping line office closed early? What if the telephone line remained busy with others seeking the same news?

Finally, the salesman got off. The central operator quickly passed through his call.

"Royal English Line. Good afternoon."

"Yes, I was calling about the SS *Peterborough*. I wondered if you had any news."

"Yes, I do have news about that ship. Let's see." He paused, apparently to consult his records. "The *Peterborough* was found off Nova Scotia this morning."

Nolan froze. Again, he envisioned bodies in the water. "*Found*? What does that mean? What did they find?"

"It means another ship spotted her and wired us her position. The *Peterborough* was just south of Cape Sable Island when she was seen."

"You mean the ship made it across unharmed?"

"Yes. They lost their wireless in a storm and couldn't communicate until about an hour ago. But yes, she reached the coast of Nova Scotia late last night and is on her way to New York. She should reach here, let me see, about seven o'clock this evening. Pier Sixty at the foot of Twentieth Street."

"Thank you! Thank you so much!"

Nolan nearly came out of his shoes racing for the door.

THE *PETERBOROUGH* TOOK a half hour to make the slow turn into its berth from the channel of the Hudson River, tugboats cautiously nudging it along. The sun had set, but the moon, in a clear sky, was up. On the pier, bright with electric lights, hundreds of relatives and friends stood behind wooden barriers in the cool night air, waiting for the gangplanks to shoot out from the ship. Nolan, having gotten there early, was able to find a place right at the barrier, some twenty yards from both the fore and aft gangplanks.

He knew passengers in the first and second class had been

politely checked by doctors at sea and would be allowed off at the pier. The poor in steerage would be taken to Ellis Island for the more rigorous examinations.

The first passengers to come off were the elderly in wheelchairs, guided by stewards. Some were wealthy enough that their limousines and carriages were allowed right down onto the pier to pick them up. The rest of the first-class passengers were the next to disembark, in twos and threes. Most were dressed in furs and expensive greatcoats. Some led pet dogs on leashes—exotic breeds such as Scottish terriers and Russian wolfhounds.

Then the second class entered the two gangplanks, recognizable by the thickness of the crowds they formed and their plainer clothes.

Ever since his school days, Nolan could spot Sheenagh instantly in any crowd. Some instinctive sense would draw him to her like a magnet to metal. For the next ten minutes, though, he did not see her and began to worry, his mind traveling to the worst possibilities. The rough weather the Royal English man mentioned—had it put her in the infirmary? Worse still, had she succumbed to sea sickness? During his own crossing, more than a dozen had died in steerage.

Then, as if an instinct guided him, he caught sight of her walking onto the ramp. It was as if her face shone with a special light. In her best long, black church coat, she was chatting with a woman beside her as she searched the crowds for him.

He shot his hand into the air and waved it back and forth until, halfway down the gangplank, she finally saw him. She smiled but barely waved in return. Instead, she fell back into conversation with the woman beside her.

It was so like Sheenagh. He never hid his feelings, wearing his heart on his sleeve with her. She always hid hers—until the intimate moments when she did not.

Then she was off the gangplank and onto the pier, walking his way. Just before reaching him, she stopped, her eyes narrowing as if trying to place him. "Don't I know you? Weren't you a boy I knew in school a long, long time ago?"

"Too long."

She rushed past the barrier and he wrapped his arms around her, hugging her tight.

"I expect a kiss right now," she whispered after a long moment in his embrace. "I've waited long enough."

As if there were no teeming crowd on the pier, no clamor, no commotion, no blaring horns of automobiles and taxicabs, no steam whistles of tugboats in the channel, no yelling voices of stevedores, no joyful shouts of one relative to another, he kissed her. As if they were alone.

In his mind, they were. They *always* were.

ABOUT THE AUTHOR

Stan Freeman was a newspaper reporter for nearly three decades. His articles appeared in more than two dozen publications, including *the San Francisco Chronicle, Seattle Times, Houston Chronicle, New Orleans Times-Picayune* and *St. Louis Post-Dispatch.* For many years, he was the science and environmental writer for the *Springfield Union-News and Sunday Republican* of Massachusetts. He also published several short stories in literary magazines and held a fiction writing fellowship from the Massachusetts Council on the Arts and Humanities.

He lives in western Massachusetts.

www.ingramcontent.com/pod-product-compliance
Lightning Source LLC
Chambersburg PA
CBHW020231260626
47156CB00002B/624